TWO BROTHERS:

The Gunslinger

Linda Lael Miller

Two Brothers:
The Gunslinger

WHEELER PUBLISHING, INC.
ROCKLAND, MA

★ AN AMERICAN COMPANY ★

Published in Large Print by arrangement with Pocket Books, a division of Simon & Schuster, Inc. in the United States and Canada.

Wheeler Large Print Book Series.

Set in 16 pt Plantin.

Library of Congress Cataloging-in-Publication Data

Miller, Linda Lael.
   Two brothers; The gunslinger / Linda Lael Miller.
      p. (large print) cm.(Wheeler large print book series)
   ISBN 1-56895-812-9 (hardcover)
   1. Frontier and pioneer life—West (U.S.)—Fiction. 2. Outlaws—West
(U.S.)—Fiction. 3. Twins—West (U.S.)—Fiction. 4. Western stories.
5. Large type books.
I. Title. II. Series
[PS3563.I41373T86   1999]
813'.54—dc21   99-031382
                                                              CIP

For Peggy Jean Knight,
who introduced me to a whole new world
and a lot of great people,
most especially, herself.
Keep on talkin' to strangers, girl.

Chapter

1

❧

June 1884

*H*E OUGHT TO MOVE ON, that was all. Bid Shay and his sweet, enterprising wife a fond farewell, saddle up his horse, and ride out of Prominence without looking back. There were a thousand places he might go—up to Montana, where he'd left a thriving cattle operation in the care of hired men, southward to San Francisco and certain women who professed to find him fair. Maybe even back East, to Chicago or Boston or New York—a man with funds to spend and invest might further himself in any of those cities, while enjoying the singular pleasures and graces of civilization.

He sighed and heaved another bag of oats up into the bed of his wagon, a small but sturdy buckboard acquired as part of the bargain when he'd purchased a local ranch nearly a year before. His brother stood watching as he worked, arms folded, one side of his mouth slanted upward in a self-satisfied grin. Shay's badge, a silver star, gleamed with all the splendor of something netted from a night sky. Shay'd been married for some time now, and the match was a contented one. He'd be a father at any time. He was proud as a rooster, and although Tristan usually found his twin's blatant good cheer cause for shared celebration, on that particular day, it chafed some tender and previously unrecognized place inside him almost raw.

"You might lend a hand," he groused, hoisting up another sack of feed from the pile of bags on the sidewalk, "instead of just standing there, watching me sweat."

Shay didn't flick an eyelash or twitch a muscle; right down to that grin—which was all the more irritating for the fact that he'd worn it on his own face often enough—he stayed the same. He didn't point out that he'd spent many an hour on Tristan's land, roping and branding calves, rounding up strays, digging post holes, stringing lines of barbed wire, driving nails into shingles on the roof of the ranch house. He didn't say anything at all.

Tristan shoved past his brother and hurled the oats into the buckboard with such force that the springs bounced and the horses, a mismatched pair of roans better suited to sod-busting, pranced and nickered and tossed their heads.

"Aislinn wants you to come to supper," Shay announced. The expression of quiet understanding in his eyes was harder to take than most any other emotion would have been, save outright pity, that is. "She's frying up a couple of chickens. You know how those brothers of hers eat. No doubt, there'll be gravy and biscuits. Mashed potatoes, too. Green beans, I reckon, boiled up with bacon and onion."

Tristan's mouth watered; he swallowed. He was tired of the food at the hotel dining room, passable though it was, and wearier still of his own sorry bachelor cooking. While he didn't lack for invitations to take evening meals and Sunday dinners in various households thereabouts, he was reluctant to accept, since such doings generally occasioned the presentation of a marriageable daughter, niece or sister. Although he fully intended to take a wife, when he found the right woman, he did not enjoy being pursued, maneuvered, manipulated and arranged. "Biscuits?" he echoed, weakening.

Knowing he'd won the skirmish, Shay pushed away from the frame of the door, took up a bag of feed and flung it into the wagon. "Biscuits," he confirmed.

Tristan swept off his hat momentarily and thrust a hand through his hair, which felt damp and gritty. He hadn't shaved in a few days, and he probably smelled of sweat and horse manure. "I'm not fit to dine at a lady's table," he said, and he heard a woeful note in his voice that shamed him not a little. He wasn't about to start sympathizing with himself at this late date.

3

Shay arched an eyebrow as he assessed the sad state of his brother's grooming. Then he glanced up at the sun, squinting against the glare. When his gaze returned to Tristan's face, he'd sobered some. "You have time enough to get yourself bathed and barbered, and I can lend you a suit of clothes."

Tristan pulled off his hat again and slapped his thigh with it. There was something about this situation he didn't care for, though he couldn't say precisely what it was. He narrowed his eyes as the nebulous sense of trouble tightened into plain suspicion. "You aren't planning to include some female in this little do, are you?"

Shay laughed. "Well, Aislinn will be there," he said. "Dorrie, too, probably. And maybe Eugenie."

"You know what I mean, damn it. Just because marriage agrees with you and Aislinn, you believe, the pair of you, that everyone *else* ought to be hitched to somebody, too."

Shay shook his head, made a clucking sound with his tongue and put a curled fist to his chest, as though to pull out a still-quavering dagger. "To think my own brother, the only real kin I have, doesn't trust me."

"You're damn right I don't."

After consulting the sun again, Shay lifted the last of the feed bags into the rig. "You're getting prickly in your old age," he commented mildly. "If you don't have a care, you might turn into one of those crusty codgers who spit tobacco in the churchyard and go

4

around with egg in their beards. See you at seven o'clock. You need a clean shirt and a pair of pants, you know where to find them."

"Thanks," Tristan said, in a tone that might have been counted surly if it hadn't been entirely justified. He climbed into the wagon box and took up the reins, setting his face toward home. His ranch house was about three miles out of town, on a high bank overlooking Powder Creek, surrounded by a thousand acres of good grassland. To the north was the Kyle property, a vast spread that he coveted with an unholy longing.

Upon his arrival, he drove the rig into the barn, climbed into the back, and unloaded the oats before jumping down to unhitch the lamentable team and settle the animals in their stalls. After feeding those broken-down creatures and the gelding, then filling all the water troughs, he made for the house, a rambling log structure, with a good rock fireplace at either end. The kitchen, dining room and parlor were all one large room, but there were four bedrooms upstairs, good, spacious ones, with lace curtains at the windows and rugs on the wide pine-plank floors. He'd taken the best and biggest for himself; it had a good wood-burning stove and a nice view of the mountains, but it was a lonely place, for all its creature comforts and uncommon size, and he passed as little time there as he could.

He carried water in from the pump in the dooryard and filled the reservoir on the stove, then built up the fire. He looked around him and sighed, wondering when he'd developed this aversion to his own company. He'd spent much of his adult life on the trail, often traveling for days with no other companion than his horse, and it had never bothered him, but instead afforded him welcome opportunity to order his thoughts. Now, even though he had work to do, hard, outdoor labor that used all there was of him, body, mind and spirit, and that he loved, now that he had money, even a family of sorts again, and should have been satisfied with his lot, he felt instead like Cain, marked and condemned to wander footloose until the end of his days.

Taking up the buckets, he went outside to pump more water, and as he walked, he whistled under his breath, grinning a little. Like as not, he was taking too solemn a view of things. He'd wash up, shave, put on clean clothes, and ride back to town. A dose of Aislinn's fried chicken would raise his spirits.

In time, he had a good bit of water heated, enough to fill the copper washtub, and he stripped down until he was naked as God's truth and gave himself a good scouring right there in the kitchen end of the house. Figuring he needed rinsing, he wrapped a sheet of toweling around his middle and headed for the yard again, meaning to douse himself with a bucket or two at the pump.

That was when he first heard the sheep.

Head dripping, one hand clasping the towel in place, Tristan stood absolutely still and listened. Yes. That bleating sound, growing ever nearer, was unmistakable.

He looked around and saw dust rising against the eastern sky in great, surging billows, like the aftermath of some apocalyptic eruption. The din was louder now, and he made out the barking of a dog, woven through in uneven stitches of noise.

The flock came over the rise behind his house then, a great, greasy-gray mob of complaining wool, heading hell-bent for the creek. Before Tristan could deal with his indignation at the intrusion, they were all around him, carrying on fit to rouse the mummies of Egypt, brushing past, raising enough grit to ruin the effects of his bath.

He watched, hot-eyed, as the sheepherder came toward him, mounted on a little spotted pony. He was a small man clad in a battered slouch hat, butternut shirt, dirty serape, indigo denim pants and scuffed boots, about as unprepossessing as he could be. The dog, some type of long-haired mix, paid Tristan no mind at all, but continued driving the sheep toward water. God knew, the beasts were probably too stupid to find it on their own.

"I guess you didn't notice the fence," Tristan said moderately, taking a hold on the pony's bridle, when the shepherd would have ridden right past him.

The trespasser's face was hidden by the shadow of his hat brim. The sheep were still spilling over the rise, and raising such a cacophony that Tristan thought his head

7

would split. That was probably why it took a moment for the soft timbre of the stranger's voice to register on his senses.

"Let go of my horse. It's thirsty and so am I."

Tristan held on, frowning. Took a tighter grasp on the towel. "That fence—"

The slouch hat fell back on its ties at a toss of the shepherd's head, revealing a head of honey-colored hair, wound into a single plait, a pair of brown eyes, thickly lashed and snapping with furious bravado, and a wide, womanly mouth. She was perhaps twenty years old, and about as ill-suited to the task she'd undertaken as it was possible to be, by his reckoning at least. Her features were refined, her bone structure was delicate; no, indeed, she was not fitted for the occupation she had chosen.

"I pulled down the fence," she said, without apology, patting a coil of frayed rope affixed to her saddle. "I won't be kept off my own land."

Tristan, still dealing with the fact that the shepherd was a woman, and the finest he'd ever seen into the account, for all that she was in sore need of tidying up, was a beat behind. The towel around his waist had taken on a whole new significance, now that his perception of the circumstances had been so drastically altered.

"Who are you?" she demanded.

He grinned, standing there in his door-yard, covered in goose bumps and sheep dust and damn little else. "That is an audacious question," he said, "given the situation. My name is Tristan Saint-Laurent, and this is *my* land."

The change in her face was barely noticeable, just a slight faltering of an otherwise resolute countenance. "You are mistaken, sir," she said. Her gaze strayed over his bare chest, took in the loincloth arrangement, and careened back up to his face. A flush stained the smooth skin beneath all that trail dirt. "Or perhaps you are simply a squatter."

"I have papers to prove I'm neither," Tristan answered, not unkindly. He was beginning to feel a little sorry for the woman, which was a laudable change from feeling sorry for himself. Of course, if she'd been a man, he might have shot her by now.

He took in the sheep, still trampling the grass in their migration to the creek, and then looked up at her again. "This is cattle country, Miss—?"

"Starbuck," she said, grudgingly. "Emily Starbuck."

He scanned the horizon, now a ragged scallop of lingering dust. The dog had gone back to collect the stragglers, but there was no sign of another horse, a wagon, or a herder on foot. Still up to his ass in sheep, Tristan was nonetheless distracted from the immediate problem. "You're not traveling all by yourself, are you?" he asked, bemused.

"Of course not," she answered, with a brittle, impatient little smile. "I've got Spud with me." With a toss of her head, she indicated the hardworking dog, then leaned forward slightly to pat the pony's gritty neck. "And Walter, here. Now, if you wouldn't mind getting out of my way, I'd like to water my horse at my stream."

Issues of ownership aside, Walter was a mare, Tristan had observed that right off, but he concluded that maybe it gave Miss Starbuck comfort to call the animal by a masculine name. "Go ahead and attend to your mount," he said. "Then you'd better come inside, where we can talk this out."

She eyed him, letting her gaze stray no lower than his breastbone this time, and blushed again. "I'm not stepping foot over that threshold or any other in the company of a near-naked man," she said with conviction, casting a glance back over one slender shoulder at the house. "Have you got a wife in there? Or a sister, at least? Somebody to serve for a chaperone?"

"No," Tristan answered, "but you're perfectly safe all the same. I am a gentleman."

Her glance was skeptical. His hold having slackened on the bridle, she reined the horse away and rode past him, through what must have been four acres of bawling woollies, toward the water.

He might have been amused by the whole situation, if it hadn't been for those blasted sheep; if they got onto his range, they'd crop the grass off flush with the ground, leaving nothing but stubble for his cattle. Those he hadn't already lost through the gap in the fence, that is. He had to get rid of Miss Star-

10

buck and her flock, soon, whether he liked the prospect or not.

Suddenly self-conscious, Tristan hurried into the house and up the stairs to his room, where he dressed hastily. His bathwater was still sitting near the kitchen floor, and he was almost as dirty as if he'd never taken a bar of soap to his hide at all, but expediency precluded all other considerations.

He nearly collided with the Starbuck woman when he wrenched open the front door and burst through it with the full momentum of urgency behind him. He gripped her shoulders, lest she fall, and in that tiny fraction of time, the merest shadow of a moment, something eternal happened. He released her as instantly as if she were made of hot metal, but it was too late. He knew he wasn't the same man who'd taken hold.

"Come inside," he said.

She seemed as shaken as he was, and he wondered if she'd felt the same strange, elemental tumult he had. "All—all right." She looked a lot smaller, now that she was down off that horse. Tristan figured she'd feel as fragile and fine-boned as a bird, if he were to touch her again. Which, of course, he wasn't about to do. Not yet, anyway.

There were no makings for tea in his bachelor's cupboard, but he did produce coffee, in fairly short order, while Miss Starbuck— he already thought of her as Emily, though he supposed that was presumptuous of him—sat primly at his plain pine table, her hands folded

11

in her lap, her outsized hat resting on the floor beside her. The infernal babble of her sheep seeped through the chinking in the sturdy log walls of the house, serving as an irritating reminder that women were women and business was business. And sheep sure as hell were sheep.

"This *is* the Eustace Cummings place, isn't it?" Emily inquired, at some length, when Tristan set a mug of steaming coffee before her.

"It was," he answered. "I bought it from him a year ago. Are you hungry? You look a little peaky."

Great tears swelled and glistened in her eyes, but she blinked them away, simultaneously shaking her head. Although she sat with her head high and her backbone rigidly straight, her despair was evident. Her hands trembled as she pulled off her leather gloves and shoved them into a pocket of the serape. "I have a marker here," she said, and stood a moment to pull a folded document from the pocket of her denims. Intrigued by the concept of a woman in pants, Tristan started wishing she'd remove the serape, and had to bring himself back to the moment by force of will. "Mr. Cummings put this place up as collateral for a debt," she went on, handing him the paper. "He defaulted, as you can see by this paper, and ownership was transferred to my uncle—"

He was touched by the earnestness of her expression. "Your uncle," he prompted, somewhat hoarsely, when she fell silent in the middle of the sentence.

12

"He died a month ago. But he left me this land and those sheep out there." She shoved the document toward him and he scanned it, and was more convinced than ever that it was a forgery. Eustace Cummings had been illiterate, but the paper bore a flowing signature. "They're all I have in the world." This last was no bid for pity, but instead a clear warning against such sentiments, should he be harboring any.

Tristan wondered if there was a blade of grass left on the acre surrounding his house; like as not, he wouldn't be able to walk to the barn without sinking to his ankles in sheep shit. He was strangely unconcerned, given how much sweat, money, hope and calculation he'd put into the place.

"You've been cheated," he said, very quietly. He wished he had some tea to offer her; the stuff seemed to perk a woman up. His mother had always taken orange pekoe when she felt melancholy, and Aislinn generally brewed the like for Dorrie, if she got to pining for her lost love, Leander.

She sat even more stiffly than before, looking miserable. Her white, even teeth were sunk into her lower lip. Presently, she said, "You will be called upon to prove that assertion, sir."

"Stop calling me sir," he ordered. "This is not a cotillion or a box social, and we're casual out here in the countryside. Where are you from, anyway?"

She sighed. "Minnesota."

"You came all the way from Minnesota

driving that flock, with just a dog to help you?"

That was when she smiled, and if Tristan had been standing, he'd have rocked back onto his heels. He damn near turned his chair over as it was, such was the impact of a simple change of expression. "I did not acquire the sheep until I reached Butte," she replied, and the smile was gone as quickly as it had arrived. The effect of its absence was quite as dramatic as that of its appearance, though in the opposite way. "You see, my uncle was my only remaining relative, and I was his ward, after a fashion. He contracted consumption, and summoned me to his side, but by the time I arrived, he was gone."

"I'm sorry," Tristan said, and he wasn't just talking. He had no blood family but Shay, and even though he'd really only known his brother for a year, he didn't like to think what it would mean to lose him. He didn't realize until she looked down at the tabletop that he'd laid his hand over hers.

She withdrew none too hastily. "Your proof?"

Tristan was momentarily baffled. "I beg your pardon?"

Emily tapped the document with the tip of a grubby index finger. "You claim to own my land. I should like to see on what authority you base your declaration, sir—er—Mr. Saint-Laurent."

"Tristan," he said, getting up. "You might as well call me by my Christian name, because I fully intend to address you as Emily."

Once again, she colored, but she let the remark pass.

He was grinning a little as he crossed the long room to the plain wood table he used as a desk. It was situated near the fireplace, a handy thing on cold nights. He took a deed from the single drawer—there was another just like it in the bank vault in town—and came unhurriedly back to where Miss Starbuck waited. Outside, the sheep continued to raise a mournful dirge.

She read the deed and if it hadn't been for the dirt covering her face, she'd have had no color at all. She swallowed hard. "Do you suppose Mr. Cummings deceived my uncle?" she asked, when an interval had passed, chopped off second by second, one tick of the mantel clock at a time.

Tristan knew only that his title to the land was legal. Looking at Emily Starbuck, sitting there in her oversized clothes, needing a bath and one of Aislinn's hearty meals even more than he did, he almost regretted his advantage. "It's possible," he said. "Cummings wouldn't be the first to cover a debt with a worthless note."

Emily sagged a little, inside all those clothes, and Tristan braced himself to catch her, fearing she was about to swoon. Instead, she rallied, her spine straight as the handle of a pitchfork. "We shall have to carry this matter before the law," she said decisively.

Tristan pointed out the date on her marker, which fell a full six months after his own cash purchase of the ranch, but he could see that even an obvious prior claim did not convince her. "I've got a few acres up in the hills where you can put those sheep," he heard himself say. "Just until everything's been decided, I mean."

She looked at him steadily for a few moments, but he knew nonetheless that she was doing everything she could to keep from breaking down to weep. He put away an urge to take her into his arms and assure her that things would work out, he'd see to it. She stood.

"That's kindly of you," she said. "If you'd just point the way—"

He was on his feet. "I'll lead you there myself." He intended to talk her into putting the sheep in the dog's care, just long enough to come to town with him and tuck into some fried chicken at Shay and Aislinn's place.

"I couldn't abandon them," she said, when he had made the suggestion, indicating the ocean of moving, baaing wool with a nod of her head. He was mounted on the gelding, and she was beside him, riding the mare she called Walter. "One cannot merely leave them to wander and round them up whenever you want. Sheep are not like cattle, Mr. Saint-Laurent."

"I do know that, ma'am," Tristan agreed good-temperedly. "And it's Tristan." He adjusted his hat and sighed, looking up at the twilight sky as he spurred the gelding into an ambling trot. The smell of live mutton filled his nostrils like an itch. "There's an old man in a line shack up ahead; I'll get him to keep an eye on the flock for you. You can't spend the night up there alone anyway."

Emily did not turn to look at him, and her face was hidden, once again, in the shadow of her hat brim. "I have not been sleeping in grand hotels since I left Butte," she said reasonably. "Spud and Walter and I, we like making our beds under the stars." She sighed. "I did expect a house to take shelter in when we arrived, though."

Tristan felt like the worst kind of brute, though he was fairly certain that hadn't been Emily's intention. "You can stay at my place. I'll bunk in the barn."

She spared him a glance. "I'll sleep near my sheep," she said. "Like I told you, they're all I have."

Tristan's attraction to this woman was equal only to the exasperation she caused him. "You can't do that. Between the bears and the mountain cats, your common drifter and some of those outlaws holed up on the Powder Creek spread, you wouldn't be safe."

"I'm not certain I'd be any better off in your ranch house. If indeed it *is* yours." She rubbed the back of her neck with one hand. "I am weary of rough accommodations, though, I must confess," she said.

They didn't speak again until they'd reached the line shack, where Tristan permitted an old hermit named John S. Polymarr to reside, in return for the occasional bit of information concerning the goings and comings of the riders up at Powder Creek.

17

Polymarr stood in his doorway, wearing an undershirt and a pair of baggy trousers held up by suspenders, watching the sheep move up the draw in a noisy V, driven relentlessly by the dog.

"You better get them critters out of here before Kyle hears tell of 'em," he said.

Tristan dismounted and removed his hat, more out of habit than real deference. His adoptive mother had been a stickler for manners. "Kyle is in the state penitentiary," he replied. "He won't be offering an opinion anytime soon, one way or the other."

Polymarr spat, let his gaze move to Emily, still mounted on her horse. "I don't hold with no sheep, myself," he said.

"I don't either," Tristan answered. "All the same, I meant to offer you five dollars to look after them for a day or two. The lady there has business in town."

The old man squinted in the gathering darkness. "That's a lady?"

Tristan felt Emily stiffen, despite the distance between them, and was glad she couldn't see that one corner of his mouth had developed a slight and intermittent twitch. He said nothing, but simply waited, thinking that she was an incredible woman, traveling all that way with only a dog and a mare and a flock of sheep for company.

"Five dollars?" Polymarr asked, and spat again.

"Two now, three more in a couple of days," Tristan said. It was a ridiculous amount of money to pay, just to get Miss Emily Starbuck to pass an evening in town with him and spend the night under his roof, but he would have given a lot more to achieve his purpose.

Polymarr rubbed his beard, only pretending to ponder the offer. The acquisitive light in his small, rheumy eyes virtually guaranteed his compliance. "Well, all right," he said, in his own good time. "But you just remember, St. Lawrence. I don't hold with no sheep."

Tristan didn't bother to correct the old man's mangling of his name, even though he greatly valued it. "Whatever your opinions," he said, placing a pair of silver dollars in the codger's hoary palm, "the count had better tally when I come back to collect those woolly wretches, or I'll take the difference out of your hide."

"Let me get my gear," Polymarr said, and went back into the shack. When he came out a few minutes later, he had a haversack over one stooped shoulder and a blanket roll under his arm. Tristan took note of the ancient pistol in the old man's belt. "What about that damn dog?" the old coot complained. "He bite or anything like that?"

"He'll tear the throat out of anything or anybody that tries to carry off one of my sheep," Emily said, without turning a hair. Tristan felt a wrench of tenderness, looking at her, thinking once again of all the miles she'd traveled on her own. It was God's own wonder she wasn't lying beside the trail someplace, dead, the world being that sort of place.

They proceeded up into the high meadow, Polymarr plodding along behind, cursing in the midst of all those caterwauling sheep, and the moon was up by the time Emily had given him instructions and commanded the dog to stay. The animal yawped and ran a few paces after her as they rode away, she and Tristan, but in the end his sense of duty kept him with the flock.

"Tell me where we are suppering," Emily said, when the sheep and Polymarr and the dog were well behind them. "I've forgotten."

"There's no fault in your memory," Tristan replied. "I don't believe I've said where we're headed. We're joining my brother and his wife in town." He hoped Aislinn had held the meal, for he did relish her fried chicken, but if she hadn't, he would take Emily to the hotel dining room. What was it, he wondered, that made him want to feed her, protect her, scrub her down and buy her every length of lace and ruffle between there and San Francisco? There were other things he wanted to do, too, but the time to think of them had not yet come.

He cleared his throat. "You didn't truly come clear from Montana all alone?"

"I did," she answered, and sounded pleased with herself, too.

"Why?" He bit the word off, like a piece of hard jerky, his head full of ugly images. He'd seen the handiwork of renegade Indians and outlaws before, along the trails and on isolated homesteads, and although he admired her grit,

20

it galled him that any woman would take such a risk.

"Why?" she echoed, her tone somewhere between incredulity and mockery. "Because it was the only way to get from there to here, that's why."

"I've made the trip myself. It isn't an easy one."

She looked at him; he felt her gaze even though he couldn't see her eyes for the hat brim. "It's been my experience," she said, "that not much is easy in this life. Some things, though—well, some things are worth fighting for."

He agreed, and it was clear to him that there was a battle ahead, sure enough. He smiled to himself. There was nothing like a good skirmish.

Chapter

2

JUST LOOKING UPON THAT sturdy house in town, with its windows spilling light into a yard where flowers surely grew, Emily thought her heart would burst with wanting such a place for her own. She had kept her spirits up all the way from Butte, more from necessity than courage, though she had her share of that to be certain, but now, all of the sudden, weariness descended upon her, wings spread and talons bared. She had been wearing the same clothes since leaving Montana, and hadn't managed more than a few washings in streams and rivers along the way. She'd probably forgotten the manners she'd taken such care to learn over the years, having lived roughly for so long, and she was bound to disgrace herself somehow.

"I can't." She didn't glance toward Tristan, but she was aware of him there beside her, all the same, sitting that gelding as though he'd been born a part of it. Her face felt hot and her chin wobbled.

"Sure you can," Tristan countered easily, just as if he knew beyond all doubt that she could. Out of the corner of her eye, she saw him swing down from the saddle and tether his mount loosely to the picket fence.

Before she could rustle up a retort, the screen door creaked open and two middle-sized boys erupted through the opening, whooping like red Indians.

"Thomas and Mark," Tristan explained. He reached up and took Emily by the waist before she could deliberate further, lifting her down, setting her lightly on her feet. "In point of fact, they're in-laws, but I think of them as nephews, most of the time."

"And the rest of the time?" Emily asked,

smoothing her trousers as though wishing and touching could make them into skirts of fine velvet, or at least clean calico. She took off the slouch hat and pegged it onto Walter's saddlehorn, then smoothed her hair with unsteady hands.

The boys were hurtling toward them over the dark grass. "The rest of the time," Tristan answered, "I pretty much accept that they're savages."

The screen door opened again, and a woman appeared. Her hair gleamed dark as onyx in the lamplight from inside, and her dress, though simple, draped her figure gracefully, for all that she was plainly with child. Once more, Emily felt the ignoble sting of envy; she turned and would have scrabbled back into the saddle and made a dash for other parts if Tristan hadn't stopped her by taking a soothing grasp on her arm.

Thomas and Mark had gained the fence and, for a beat, they were quiet, peering at Emily in the faulty glimmer of a waning moon. "Who's that?" one of them inquired.

"Miss Emily Starbuck," Tristan said, as formally as if he'd been presenting her at some grand ball, "meet Thomas Lethaby, there on the left. That's his brother, Mark, on the right."

"You're a girl?" the one called Mark wanted to know. He seemed skeptical.

"Howdy," Thomas said, simultaneously elbowing his sibling in the ribs.

"Boys! Come inside, this minute," the dark-haired woman commanded, with loving authority. She stood partway down the walk, and the children obeyed her reluctantly, casting backward glances as they went, while Tristan opened the gate and stood aside to let Emily precede him. She had to force herself through for, drawn though she was, a part of her still wanted to bolt.

"Are we too late for supper?" Tristan asked, addressing the woman. There was a smile in his voice, and a degree of caring too pure and quiet to be without meaning. He'd swept off his hat, as well, holding it loosely in one hand.

The lady of the house laughed. "You know you could turn up in the middle of the night, looking for a meal, and never go away hungry." She put out a hand to Emily. "Good evening," she said. "I'm Aislinn McQuillan."

Emily responded with a handshake and gave her name shyly.

"Won't you come in?" Aislinn asked. By that time, she'd curved an arm around Emily's waist and was gently propelling her toward the house. A man stood on the porch now, leaning with his hands braced against the white-washed railing, the warm light glowing golden in his fair hair. Although Emily could make out only the outline of his frame and a general sense of his manner, she recognized right away that he was a twin to Tristan.

Emily was secretly mortified by the state of her person, particularly her clothing, as she passed along the walk, up the steps, into the house. She regretted letting Tristan persuade her to accompany him here and, at one and the same time, yearned to be taken into the laughter, into the light, if only for a single evening. Like a ragged and piteous wayfarer, warming her hands at a friendly fire. "I've been traveling for many weeks," she said, in an effort to explain the trousers, the serape, the collarless shirt made for a man.

"With sheep," Tristan added, in the entryway.

The other man gave a low whistle of exclamation.

"This," Aislinn said, smiling as she turned to indicate Tristan's precise replica, "is my husband, Shamus McQuillan. We call him Shay."

"Sheep," Shay marveled, as though he'd not heard of such an animal before.

A table was set in the dining room, with candles and china and silver shining fit to dazzle the eye. There was nary a sign of Thomas and Mark; Emily suspected they were looking on from some hidden vantage point, though. She couldn't help a small smile, nervous as she was.

"This way," Tristan said, before Emily had to ask for a place to freshen up. He took a light hold on her arm and led her on through the dining room into the spacious kitchen behind. After fetching a basin and a ladle from the mud room, he lifted a lid on the side of the huge black cookstove, trimmed in gleaming chrome, and soon there was hot water. Soap.

Emily yearned toward those plain refinements just as she had toward the house itself; she removed the serape, at a gesture from Tristan, and washed her face and hands as sedately as she could. Her every instinct bade her plunge into that basin, splashing exuberantly and shouting for joy, so welcome was the prospect of being even moderately clean again.

When Tristan led her back to the table, where his brother and sister-in-law waited, talking in low voices, she felt almost presentable. She had decided that, in this one instance at least, she would suspend all thought of her troubles and allow herself to enjoy a pleasant meal in this merry and benevolent place. For much of her life, she had lived in the future, plotting and planning and worrying, anticipating and preparing, but tonight, by conscious choice, she would confine herself strictly to the moment.

It proved dangerously easy to pretend that she had a place in the midst of this glad gathering, that she truly belonged. She forgot her dreary life in Minnesota, where she had been the child bride of a man her uncle's age, and subsequently a widow, forgot the difficulties she had had to face on her arrival in Butte, and the long, lonely and perilous trip overland to Prominence. For a little while, in her mind at least, her clothes befitted a woman, her future was a thing of bright assurance, and she had every right to enjoy the laughter and talk crisscrossing the table.

Only when the evening was drawing to a close, and the four of them were taking rich coffee from china cups, did the subject of sheep come up again.

"There will be trouble when the ranchers hear about that flock," Shay predicted. Although he was looking at Tristan when he spoke, Emily knew the comment was directed at her. After all, the sheep were hers.

"I believe Emily expected to run them on her own land," Tristan said. His glance touched her, from across the table, as effective as a caress. "She was cheated—probably by Eustace Cummings himself."

Shay sighed sympathetically. "That old swindler," he said, with a sort of desultory affection. "The church was packed to the shingles at his funeral, but I suspect most folks just wanted to make sure he was really in the box."

"Shay!" Aislinn scolded, but her husband merely grinned and covered her hand with his, the thumb playing over her knuckles. She blushed prettily, but made no move to pull away.

Once again, Emily felt envious. In four sterile years of marriage to Cyrus Oxlade, she had never been touched so gently. Indeed, she had been a servant, not a wife. A possession, not a companion. Aislinn, she could see, was a full partner to Shay, and he clearly adored her.

"In any case," Tristan said, "Emily expected to find a house and land waiting for her here. Instead, she found me."

The words gave Emily an odd little thrill, though they shouldn't have done. She couldn't have spoken then for anything; it was as if she were strangling on her own tongue. *Instead, she found me.*

Aislinn passed her a kindly, knowing look. "Well, what will you do now?" she asked, in a practical tone, bare of prejudice or any preconception of justice.

Emily found her voice, but it came dry from her throat. "I guess I'll speak with a lawyer," she said uneasily. It amounted to a bald challenge, but still, it was the truth. She wasn't going to take Tristan Saint-Laurent's word that the ranch was his; she couldn't afford to do that. She had, after all, nowhere else to go, and some two hundred sheep to look after.

"You're welcome to stay here with us," Aislinn said, her friendliness undiminished. "Until everything is decided, I mean. We have plenty of room."

Emily did not dare to look at Tristan for fear of what she might see in his face. "Mr. Saint-Laurent has been kind enough," she said boldly, "to offer me the use of his—of the house, temporarily."

" 'Mr. Saint-Laurent'?" Shay echoed, in the same half-amused tone in which he'd said "Sheep?" earlier.

There was a short silence, then Tristan pushed back his chair and stood. "It's getting late," he said, "and I'm sure Emily is tired."

"I'm sure she is," Shay agreed mildly, standing too. Being nearest, he drew back Emily's chair before going on to perform the same service for his wife. Emily could not decide whether or not she liked Shamus

28

McQuillan, and though she knew him to be almost an exact duplicate of Tristan, physically at least, she saw marked yet not easily definable differences between the two men. As alike as they were, she was sure she would have no difficulty in telling them apart.

"Thank you," Emily said earnestly, to Aislinn, as Tristan ushered her quickly toward the door. "I can't think when I've had a finer meal, or a more congenial evening." That much was certainly true.

Aislinn was looking at Tristan, and a small smile lurked at one corner of her mouth. "I daresay we'll be seeing a great deal more of each other, Miss Starbuck," she said, a moment before her gaze slid back to meet Emily's. There was a merry sparkle in her eyes, part mischief, part welcome.

"I'll be quite busy with my sheep, I expect," Emily said, with some regret. They were on the walk by then, and she was a little breathless, keeping up with Tristan's pace.

"Good night," he called, without looking back.

Perhaps half an hour later, they arrived at the ranch house Emily had expected to own, by virtue of her uncle's bequest. It was dark, and the moonlight was thin. Tristan led the way inside, entering by the front door, and lit a lamp waiting on a table pushed up against the wall.

Emily hesitated on the threshold.

"Come in," Tristan said patiently. Quietly. "I'm harmless, I promise you."

Instinct told Emily that he was *anything* but harmless—he wore the .45 on his hip with too much ease for that, and his smile alone was a weapon—and yet something deep within urged her to trust him, in this one instance at least. She stepped through the opening.

He cocked a thumb toward the stairs. "Take the big room, at the end of the hallway. I'll bring up a couple of buckets of hot water and be on my way."

She yearned for any semblance of a bath, and the thought of a real bed to sleep in made her throat tight with gratitude and wonder. "Why are you being so kind to me?" she asked. "I still believe this is my land—my house." She had to keep believing, because without that, she had nothing.

He gave her another one of those devastating grins, and as far as Emily was concerned, it constituted an unfair advantage. "I see no reason to be *un*kind," he said. "If it turns out that you have a legal claim on this ranch—which you don't—I'll concede the point gracefully. In the meantime, you need somewhere to be."

She had gotten as far as the base of the stairs, and she paused there, one hand curled around the top of the newel post. "I could have stayed in town, with your brother and his wife," she reminded him.

He sighed, lit another lamp, and handed it to her for the ascent to the second floor. "You would have been too far away from your sheep," he said, and it sounded so reasonable that Emily had nodded and covered most of the distance between the foyer and the door of the assigned bedroom before it struck her that Tristan's concern for the welfare of her flock was at plain odds with his own interests as a cattleman.

Not that Emily believed that sheep and cattle could not coexist, as many ranchers claimed. Granted, rams and ewes chewed grass right down to the roots when they grazed, but if the flock was confined to Emily's own acreage, there was no cause for her neighbors to be concerned. Unless, of course, she didn't *have* any land, in which case she did not know what she would do.

She turned the knob and entered the room Tristan had offered. He had told her it was his, and yet she was unprepared for the dizzying sense of intimacy that swept over her when she caught sight of the spacious bed where he slept, the wardrobe where he no doubt stored his clothing, the washstand where he performed his ablutions, night and morning....

The lamp trembling a little in her hand, Emily closed the door carefully behind her. She set the light on a bureau, bare except for a hairbrush with an ivory handle and a small photographic likeness of a man and woman standing in front of a log house. At variance with most such subjects, they were both smiling, and each had an arm around the other.

The sight made Emily smile, too, and filled her with a strange, poignant affection. As a defense, against that ungovernable emotion rather than against Tristan himself, she carried the room's one chair to the door and propped it under the latch.

She pulled the serape off over her head and hung it carefully from a peg on the wall, then went to sit on the edge of the thick mattress. She wondered uncharitably if the bed belonged to Tristan, or if it might properly be viewed as a part of the Eustace Cummings estate. A brisk knock at the door interrupted her musings, and she stiffened, as though caught in some act of wrongdoing. "Yes?"

Tristan spoke from the hallway. "There was some hot water left in the reservoir," he said. "I'm leaving it out here. You'll find towels and soap in the cabinet under the washstand, and you're welcome to use one of my shirts for a nightgown if you want."

Emily stood, somewhat shakily, her face warm. She was glad for the door between them, not just for virtue's sake, but because it served to hide her state of renewed embarrassment. The prospect of wearing a garment belonging to Tristan against her bare skin, of sleeping on sheets that might still bear the invisible imprint of him, the scent and the shape, nearly overwhelmed her.

She would have been far better off, she concluded, too late, to pass the night on the ground, with her sheep nearby and only Spud to protect her.

"Thank you very much," she called, in a tone as even and steady as she could make it.

She moved the chair but stood pressed to the door, waiting, listening for his retreating footsteps. When she heard him descending the stairs, she stepped quickly out into the hallway to collect the two buckets of steaming water.

Half an hour later, scrubbed and clad in a clean cotton shirt that reached almost to her knees, Emily sat cross-legged in the middle of the bed, grooming her hair with Tristan's brush. The rainwater scent of him was all around her, just as she had feared it would be, but the reality proved comforting, rather than worrisome. She had no sensible reason to be frightened; if her host had meant to take unseemly advantage, he'd already had more than ample opportunity to do so. No, it was not him she was afraid of, but something in herself. Some longing, some unmet need she could not define. Her marriage had done nothing at all to prepare her for what she felt in the presence, even the *shadow* of the presence, of Tristan Saint-Laurent.

After re-plaiting her hair, she turned down the wick on the lamp until the light was snuffed out, then crawled beneath the covers and stretched. She did not expect to sleep, but exhaustion must have claimed her right away, for the next thing she knew, sunlight was prodding, red-gold, at her eyelids.

It was another moment before Emily fully realized that she was not lying on the hard, cold ground, fully dressed and tangled in her bedroll, but upon a nest of the softest feathers.

And sheets—cool, clean, linen sheets, still crisp with newness.

Tristan Saint-Laurent's bed. The quilt might have been ablaze, so quickly was she out from under the covers and standing on the hooked rug, her breathing rapid and shallow, her heart pounding.

She closed her eyes. Instructed herself to be calm. It wasn't as if Tristan was *in* the bed, after all, or even in the room.

Hastily, she shook out her clothes and dressed, wishing for more hot water in which to wash her face. Moving the chair from under the knob, she peered out into the hallway, in one direction and then the other. No sign of anyone.

She made her way downstairs, saw that there were cheerful blazes crackling in the fireplaces at either end of the long, sparsely furnished room. Tristan was nowhere in sight, although she found a pot of fresh-brewed coffee waiting on the stovetop. She took an enamel mug from a set of open shelves and, using the tail of her serape for a pot holder, poured a generous portion. Her stomach rumbled, but she tried to ignore it. Bad enough that she was beholden for supper and a night of shelter, not to mention the engagement of Mr. Polymarr to look after her flock. Breakfast could only make things worse. Besides, she fully intended to take the matter to law, and when the judge decreed that this land was hers, she would thank Tristan for his cordial treatment, then ask him to pack his belongings and leave immediately.

The door opened while she was still mired in these thoughts, and Tristan came in, carrying an armload of wood, which he tossed into the box beside the stove with an exuberant clatter. His grin was winsome. "I brew a fine cup of coffee," he said. "Unfortunately, that's all I can make that's fit to offer company."

"I can cook," Emily was flabbergasted to hear herself say.

"Good," Tristan answered, dusting his hands together. Before Emily could correct any misimpression she might have given him, he was out the door again, leaving it open behind him. She stood on the threshold watching him walk toward what was probably a springhouse. *Her* springhouse, she reminded herself, but it didn't help much, staking mental claims. She was having a very hard time thinking of this man as an opponent, let alone a prospective enemy, but in reality he was both. This was probably her one chance to have a real home, and he had the power to thwart that dream.

Momentarily, he came out of the little outbuilding, carrying a lidded stoneware crock under one arm, along with something wrapped in cheesecloth.

"Eggs," he said, tapping the side of the crock for emphasis. "I bought them yesterday at the general store." He indicated the gauzy package with a nod. "And this is bacon."

Emily's mouth watered. She'd been living on hardtack and beans since she'd left Butte, and she'd counted herself lucky to have that much, given the state of her late uncle's finances. He'd had nothing but the sheep and a marker for a thousand acres of land—this land, on which she stood. She turned and went inside to set a skillet on the stove, telling herself that cooking one meal for Saint-Laurent was the least she could do, given the hospitality he'd offered.

"Please cut that bacon into thin slices," she said, over one shoulder. "And wash your hands first, if you don't mind."

Tristan executed a salute that might have seemed cocky if it hadn't been for the smile in his blue eyes. "Yes, ma'am," he said. She heard him leave, watched through the window while he scrubbed at the pump, using bright yellow soap.

Twenty minutes later, they were seated across the table from each other, sharing a meal. Emily felt a bit dizzy, and for a brief and unnerving interval, she could not recall how she'd gotten from the decision to leave without accepting anything else from her charming adversary to this present, companionable moment. It was as if she had been bewitched.

"What did you do in Minnesota?" Tristan asked. He'd eaten with good appetite, but now he seemed to have lost interest in the food.

Emily drew a deep breath and let it out slowly. "I was married," she said.

He considered her in silence for a while. Why, she wondered, did she want to tell him everything—how Cyrus had never been a real husband to her, how she'd sometimes felt so lonesome in the night that she'd curled up in a ball on her bed and held her belly with both arms, like somebody dying?

"What became of your husband?" he asked. His tone was easy, moderate, but he cared about her answer, she could see that in his eyes.

Emily looked down at her hands. Even though she wore leather gloves every day, her skin was callused and reddened, her nails broken. "He died," she said. "Just collapsed one day, out in the fields."

"I'm sorry," Tristan said, and for some reason it shamed her, his sympathy.

She met his gaze. "It's your turn," she told him briskly. "You and Shay McQuillan are clearly twins. Why do you have different names?" *Who is that smiling couple in the daguerreotype upstairs?*

"That's a long and rather remarkable story. To be brief, Shay and I were born on a wagon train, somewhere in the Rockies, to a young couple making their way west. Our father— his name was Patrick Killigrew—was killed by Indians the same day we came into the world, and our mother, Mattie, died that night. A family called McQuillan took Shay in, while I went on with the Saint-Laurents."

It was indeed an amazing tale. "Did you know where he was while you were growing up?"

Tristan shook his head. "My mother—my adoptive mother, that is—told me what had happened when she took sick a few years back, and gave me a remembrance book that belonged to Mattie. I found out where Shay was by other means, but I might never have come here if I hadn't been looking for somebody else." For the first time since she'd met him, and then just for the briefest moment, Tristan looked uncertain. "I meant to move on, once I'd taken care of business."

Emily felt uncomfortable. Although Tristan Saint-Laurent seemed affable, and even boyish, she sensed that there were uncharted depths to his nature, knew somehow that the currents could be dark and treacherous. "Business?"

His smile was dazzling, like a sudden show of sunshine on a cloudy day. "I got what I came for," he said. "And I found out I liked having a family again."

Emily waited. She wouldn't ask about the likeness in the frame on Tristan's bureau top, wouldn't ask if he'd ever had a wife and children of his own.

"Shay and I butt heads on a fairly regular basis," he went on, and a rueful light danced in his eyes. "All the same, it's a fine thing to have a brother. Were you close to your uncle?"

The question caught Emily quite unprepared. She had never really been close to anyone, except for some of the characters in the books she read and the made-up people she turned to when she was alone too long, or scared. "Well, no," she said, in a surprised tone. "My father died before I was born, and my mother passed on soon after. I boarded on a neighboring farm—that's where I learned to cook." She blushed. "I don't usually talk so much." At least she hadn't blurted out that the farm was Cyrus's, and she'd joined the household to take care of his ailing wife, Mary.

He laughed and glanced at her empty plate. "Or eat so much, I reckon."

Now it was Emily who laughed. She'd consumed twice as much food as Tristan had, and she could have eaten more, if the platter between them hadn't been scraped bare. The ease she felt frightened her more than all those nights alone on the trail had done, and she composed herself, bit her lower lip, sat up very straight in her chair.

"What is it?" Tristan asked, his voice quiet. It might be her undoing, that gentle voice.

She stood, managed a wooden smile. Tristan rose, too, and faced her over the table. "I must get back to my sheep, Mr. Saint-Laurent. I appreciate your generosity, but we are adversaries, aren't we?"

"Are we?" he countered.

She retreated a step, for no other reason than that she wanted so much to draw nearer to him. "Yes," she said, and the word came out sounding strangled and dry. "Yes." With that, she made for the door, open to the crisp midsummer morning.

"Miss Starbuck," he said.

She looked back, saw him standing in the kitchen doorway, arms folded, one shoulder braced against the jamb. "You'll need your horse," he said reasonably.

She stopped, glanced questioningly toward the barn.

Tristan pushed away from the door frame and ambled toward her. He had left his hat inside, and the sun caught fire in his hair. "I put Walter out to pasture," he said.

"What?"

"The mare is worn out, Emily."

Through difficulty after difficulty, Emily had kept her chin up and her eyes dry. Now, in the face of Tristan's determined goodwill, she felt like bursting into tears. "Walter is a mare?" she asked, partly because she wanted to know, and partly because she needed a few moments to shore up her backbone.

"Yep," Tristan answered, with another crooked grin. His arms were folded again, and his eyes were narrowed against the cool brightness of the morning. "I don't mind making you the loan of a horse," he said, "if you'll take one of the nags that usually pull my buckboard."

The loan of a horse, like breakfast, was more than she wanted to accept, but she knew Walter must be exhausted. God knew, she was, but she had sheep to see to, Mr. Polymarr notwithstanding, and Spud, her one true friend, would surely be wondering where his mistress had gone. "I suppose it's too far to walk," she said.

Tristan laughed again. "Not if you don't mind spending half the day making the trip," he replied.

Emily was beginning to understand the concept of killing with kindness. "All right!" she cried, in humorous consternation, flinging up her hands. "I'll borrow a horse!"

Tristan shook his head, and although he made an effort to look solemn, amusement lingered around his mouth. He cocked a thumb toward the barn. "Help yourself," he said. Then he turned and walked back to the house, whistling under his breath, while she stood in her tracks, staring after him.

Chapter

3

AFTER SADDLING ONE OF THE plodding animals she found in the barn—neither of them looked fit to ride, if you wanted her opinion—Emily set out for the sheep camp in the hills. She might have been a greenhorn in every other respect, but she had a fine sense of direction, and she remembered each turn and twist in the trail that led up into the hills, where her flock was grazing.

For all her skill at finding her way, the ride took almost an hour. Emily was captivated, and kept stopping to look back over the land and admire the sparkling ribbon of water that was the creek, the stout and spacious log house with its mortar chinking and double chimneys, a mansion by frontier standards, the abundant, waving grass, miles and miles of it, it seemed, rippling and flowing in the breeze like some fragrant green sea. Tristan's cattle dotted the landscape as well, but she didn't begrudge them space in the promised land. In their way, they belonged as surely as the trees and stones, the ground and sky.

It was Tristan who didn't fit, Emily reasoned, with some sorrow. When Spud came streaking toward her, barking a joyous welcome and setting the sheep to bleating, she turned from her worries and jumped down to ruffle the dog's pointed ears.

Mr. Polymarr, who had been stretched out under a tree, pondering the inside of his ancient hat, scrabbled to his feet, roused by the ruckus, however belatedly, and cursing like a sailor. Spud, ever the gentleman, growled in disapproval.

The old man waved a dismissive hand at the dog as he trundled over to where Emily stood. "Mornin'," he said, miser-like, as though it cost him to part with even that one word.

"Good morning, Mr. Polymarr," Emily said, amused. She scanned the sheep, knew in that one practiced glance that they were all there, safe and well, if considerably spent from the long trek south. They would need all that was left of the summer grass to prepare for the long, snowy winter awaiting them, she reflected, but in the spring the lambs would come and, soon after, the adult animals could be sheared, their wool sold. A few, but only a few, were to be sold for mutton.

She had by no means forgotten that the cold months, not to mention Tristan Saint-Laurent and a host of other problems, stood between the difficult present and the first profits.

"I didn't expect to see you for a while," Polymarr said, rubbing his white-bristled chin, then spitting. "How do you tolerate these critters, carryin' on the way they do?"

Emily laughed. "They'll quiet down in a few minutes," she said. "Hearing Spud barking like that, they probably thought they were going to be moved again, poor things."

Polymarr sidestepped along beside Emily as she approached the grove of trees where he had made camp the night before. "I was kind of hopin' to stay on, at least until St. Lawrence gives me them other three dollars I got comin'."

The view from the knoll was breathtaking, just as Emily had expected. She stood gazing at it, stricken to the heart by an unrecognized emotion, neither joy nor sorrow, but something made up of both, and as intense as either. One hand shaded her eyes from the sun. "I suppose I could use your help," she said, her throat thick. She imagined the valley in autumn, rimmed in gold and crimson and orange, and in winter, muffled beneath a layer of clean, glittering snow. Spring would bring the first pale grass, the crocuses and dandelions and a riot of wildflowers. How could she turn her back on such a place?

"You may stay if you wish. Just be warned that I cannot—and will not—pay you the same exorbitant wages you're getting from Tristan."

Polymarr squinched up his bulbous nose, baffled. "Tristan?"

"Mr. St. Lawrence," she said, with a little laugh, aware that if she said "Saint-Laurent" he wouldn't know who she was talking about. "I'm offering twenty dollars a month, and you won't see any of that before spring."

"What I *don't see* is, I don't see no wagon. I ain't takin' to the trail with no means of shelter. 'Round about October, it'll commence to snowin', and it won't let up much afore April." He studied her with a sort of hopeful speculation. " 'Less you're headed south, o' course."

Emily sighed. "I'm not going anywhere," she said, gazing toward the distant ranch house. "I intend to settle right here, on this land. If you choose to hire on, you can either stay in the line shack or make a place for yourself in one of the outbuildings on the ranch."

Polymarr's Adam's apple went up and down, galloping the length of his neck like an ostrich in a trench. His filmy eyes were narrowed, and he pointed one scrawny and none too clean index finger at Emily. "You couldn't keep sheep around here, miss, even with St. Lawrence's say-so. The other ranchers won't put up with it for a minute. Fact is, I've been expectin' 'em to come in here shootin' since last night, and I got nary a wink of sleep for imaginin' my demise and sayin' my prayers, lest my soul go astray 'twixt here and heaven."

"I see." Along her slow route down from Montana, Emily had encountered quite a few ranchers, some with small spreads, some with large. They'd watched her coldly as she passed through and by their towns, sometimes touching a hand to a hat brim in acknowledgment, but never smiling or extending any kind of welcome. The women had kept a careful distance, always, peering at her from behind fluttering curtains, as though she were an oddity, too dangerous to approach. Once or twice, men on horseback had surrounded her and the sheep, "escorting" the flock through their territory without even a pretense of friendliness. She'd been an outcast then, and it seemed now that things would be no different in Prominence. Her dejection was profound, for she wanted nothing so much as a home, though she wasn't precisely surprised.

"You got a gun, miss?" Polymarr pressed. "Somethin' to protect yourself with?"

She showed him the .38 caliber pistol in the holster under her serape. She had a cartridge belt, too, but she dreaded having to shoot anyone or anything, for she'd taken little practice, being possessed of a Christian aversion to violence. Anyhow, the noise of gunfire invariably upset her nerves.

"Not much of a weapon," the old man said. "Still, I guess it'd be better'n nothin'. You mean to stay around these parts, ma'am, you best get yourself a rifle. One of them carbines, maybe, like they use in the army."

Emily shuddered. "Maybe," she agreed,

45

somewhat forlornly. She hadn't dared to attempt the long southward journey unarmed, but she had no plans to become another Annie Oakley, either. Her dearest hope was to make a place for herself in the valley by peaceful means; she wanted a home, like Aislinn McQuillan's, a place of love and laughter, of light and warmth, with bright, pretty dishes on shelf and table, and plenty of hot water always near at hand. It didn't seem like so much to ask, but she had met with discouragement too many times in her life to believe that dreams were ever assured of coming true, however plain and ordinary they might be.

She drew a deep and somewhat shaky breath. There was nothing to do, as far as she could determine, but press on.

Sure enough, at least fifty yards of his fence lay flat, the posts pulled right up out of the ground. From the looks of the tracks in the dirt, half his cattle must have been on the lookout for a chance to make for Powder Creek and mix in with the Kyle herd. They'd practically stampeded, those miserable animals, completely obliterating all sign of the sheep Emily had driven in from the other direction.

Until then, Tristan had run the operation alone, except for occasional help from Shay and old John Polymarr, but it had become clear to him of late that he'd have to hire on a couple of cowpunchers if he wanted to make any real headway. He preferred his own counsel, being a man with secrets to keep, and independent into the bargain, but he'd reached a pass where a choice had to be made. He could take to the trail again, or he could stay and put down roots for the first time since leaving the home place in Montana, after his folks died.

Muttering a curse, he spurred the gelding over the broken fence line and began following the trail of hoofprints. About a hundred yards along, the path began to fan out in every direction but back toward home. Tristan held to the center, moving toward the high meadow that lay ahead and above. He was out in the open, leaning into the climb with the horse, and he would have preferred not to be so vulnerable. The cattle hadn't been accommodating enough to choose a way that would have suited him better.

He sensed the riders before he saw them, drew the .45 and let it rest easily in his hand. There were two of them, one on a black and white paint, one on a bay stallion, and they'd probably been watching him for a while, because they carried their rifles across the pommels of their saddles, instead of in the scabbards, as peaceable men might do.

"This is private land," one of them said. His tone was neither neighborly nor threatening, and he had a long, solemn face, like an undertaker or a preacher fond of hellfire.

Tristan sighed. He supposed the prudent thing would have been to stop where he was, but they were on top of the rise, and he was damned if he'd let them have that advantage. Reaching the top of the hill, he nodded a greeting, the .45 resting loose in his hand.

"I guess you don't hear too good," said the man on the paint. He was hefty, and not without vanity, if his waxed mustache and slicked-down hair were any indication. The ruddy flush under his skin vouched for an uncertain disposition. "My partner here said this is private land."

Tristan repressed a sigh. Even though he was practically lounging in the saddle, he could have dropped both men before they managed to raise their rifles, and he felt the old, not-unpleasant quiver of excitement in the pit of his belly at the prospect. It was not a thing he liked knowing about himself.

"Some of my cattle've strayed onto the Powder Creek spread. But I expect you know that." He paused. "I've come to fetch them back. I expect you know that, too."

The ranch hands looked at each other. By tacit agreement, or perhaps long habit, Handlebar sat there choking on his tongue, while his companion did the talking. "You ain't got no cattle here," he said, with a slight motion of the rifle. *Get out,* the gesture said, clear as rainwater.

Undaunted, Tristan cocked the .45 and swung the barrel forward in a motion as natural to him as turning over in his sleep. "I'm not looking for trouble," he said evenly. "On the other hand, I don't mind a lively skirmish now and again, and I'm a pretty fair shot. Wouldn't it be simpler—not to mention safer—to let me look for my stock and ride out again?"

"Shoot him for trespassin'," said Handlebar. Evidently, he just couldn't withhold his opinion.

"His brother's the marshal," the other man pointed out.

"And this here's the fella that shot off half the boss's ear and got him sent away to the state penitentiary." Handlebar regarded Tristan with genuine hatred.

"Now, don't give me all the credit," Tristan protested affably. "Shay did his part, along with twelve good men and a sensible judge."

Veins bulged at the heavy man's temples, but his companion, having the cooler head, prevailed. "We've got a score to settle with you, Saint-Laurent, and with your brother, too. Billy's dead on account of you, and the boss is doin' hard time—an old man like him—and we ain't gonna forget that. But we'll have our day, right enough. Meantime, we'll check our herds for your brand, and cut out any that might have strayed."

"I'd like to go along," Tristan said. It wasn't a request, of course, even though it might have sounded like one, but a statement of intent. A man who didn't protect his stock, whatever the risks, would soon be out of business.

The other riders lowered their rifles, but Tristan waited until both guns were tucked into their respective scabbards before putting away the .45. He was watchful, but in his long career he'd learned to predict what a man meant to do next, and he was fairly certain these two didn't intend to put him to the test. At least, the smart one didn't.

He rode between them, and a little behind, the three horses moving at an easy trot. For some reason he couldn't put a finger on, Emily Starbuck came to mind, and he reflected that predicting a man's actions was one thing, and divining a woman's was quite another. He'd explained to her that the land south of Powder Creek was his, and showed her the proof, but that didn't mean she'd take her square mile of squalling mutton and strike out for new horizons. Even though he would have willed those sheep to perdition if he could have, he half hoped Miss Starbuck would stand toe-to-toe and fight.

He had no doubt that he'd come out the winner, in the long run, but in the meantime the competition would be a spirited one, and thus very entertaining.

He smiled in anticipation as he and the cowpunchers rode through a stand of birch and aspen trees, still climbing, though the slope was gentler now. When they reached the crest of the hill, the high meadow was visible, and William Kyle's sprawling stone house loomed, with the mountains and the sky for a backdrop.

Tristan did admire that house, and where before he'd tormented himself with impossible images, in which Aislinn was its mistress, and he its master, that day he couldn't think beyond Emily. She was the one he envisioned, presiding over the place, wearing a fancy dress, her hair pinned loosely at her nape. He could even picture her carrying a child, his child, her face glowing with health and pride.

He'd made inquiries in town, with Kyle's lawyer, where the property was concerned—the old man wasn't likely to need the place again, and he'd left no heirs—but it didn't seem prudent to mention the subject in the presence of his escorts, them being so prickly and all.

An Indian woman, beautiful despite her barrel body and moon-shaped face, stepped onto the porch to shake out a rug. She looked at Tristan with bland curiosity, then went back inside the house. By then his presence had drawn notice from other quarters, and he thought it judicious to pay closer attention to the men watching him from the corral fence. That there were other eyes looking on as well, he did not doubt, but there was no fear in him. His adoptive father had always said he could have done with a few more qualms, where confrontations were concerned, but there had been something reckless in him in those days, and he hadn't mellowed overmuch in the interim.

He had no conscious wish to die, but he'd done a few things in the past that made him wonder if some part of him wasn't courting death. While he was ruminating on that possibility, he kept an eye on the men around him, prepared to summon the .45 if the need arose.

"Our good neighbor here claims some of his

51

cattle have found their way onto Mr. Kyle's land," said the lean-faced man, to the half-dozen cowboys who drew nigh, all of them mounted and armed. Tristan had already figured out that he'd been at Powder Creek for a long while and, given his air of authority, he was almost surely the foreman. "You boys look after him, and make sure he don't meet with calamity whilst he's in our care."

The ranch hands didn't respond. They were sizing Tristan up, which was fair enough, because he was taking their measure, too. They looked like no-accounts to him, collecting wages, passing through, but having no particular loyalty to Kyle himself. He was always careful not to put too much stock in hasty judgments, but he trusted his gut far more than his eyes and ears, and so far, it hadn't offered an opinion. Which probably meant they weren't dangerous, unless you were stupid enough to turn your back on them, of course. Tristan admitted to a fair number of shortfalls in his nature, but stupidity was not among them. As before, he rode a pace or two behind, and presently found himself overlooking a considerable herd.

There were three riders to his left, three to his right. The youngest, a doe-eyed kid barely out of knickers, wheeled his horse around and approached, taking visible care not to make any sudden moves.

Tristan bit back a smile. He supposed the boy valued those shell-like ears of his, and didn't want their shape altered.

"What's your brand?" the kid asked. He sounded testy.

The mark was a crescent moon, and Tristan said as much, though he was sure it was common knowledge. Prominence wasn't all that big a place, and there were no more than a dozen ranches within a fifty-mile radius.

"You just stay right here," said the lad, "and we'll cut out your cattle."

"Like I said before," Tristan replied dryly, "I plan to take an active part in that process, thanks all the same."

There was no further argument, though the boy was plainly simmering with opinions to which he didn't quite dare give utterance. He swept off his hat, dragged a forearm across his brow, and spurred his horse toward the cattle grazing placidly below. The other riders followed at a slower pace, and Tristan fell in behind them.

They cut out forty-odd head of beef over the course of two hours, and while Tristan suspected there were more, he decided to content himself with what he'd recovered, for the moment at least. The boy, who grudgingly admitted that he was called Fletcher—he didn't say if it was his first name or his last—was nominated by the others to help Tristan drive the cattle back over the broken fence line onto his own land.

"You like working for that outfit?" Tristan inquired. He was setting up the posts Emily had pulled out by that time, using a flat rock to pound them into the ground. Fletcher lingered, without saying why, still mounted and looking fretful.

The boy shrugged. "It pays a decent wage," he answered. "I get my grub and a place to sleep."

Tristan spoke calming words to the gelding, who'd grown fitful from the pounding, before pausing to look up into Fletcher's face. "I could use a good hand around here, if you're interested."

No smile. "I might be. How many men you got workin' for you now?"

Tristan grinned. "Just you, I'm afraid. You'd have the bunkhouse all to yourself."

Fletcher glanced back over one shoulder as if to see if he'd been trailed from the Powder Creek spread, then met Tristan's gaze straight on. "What makes you think you can trust me?" he asked.

"I didn't say I trusted you," Tristan answered and, tossing aside the rock, he gripped one of the fence posts in both hands and gave it a good wrench, to make sure it was stable. It was. "I said I needed help. Either you want the job, or you don't. That's all we have to discuss right now."

"I'd have to have a horse. This one belongs to Kyle."

"I'll provide a cow pony."

"I can shoot, too."

Tristan suppressed a grin. "That's fine," he said, "but I hope you won't have use for that skill." He murmured a few soothing words to the gelding and mounted, anxious to be gone.

Miss Emily Starbuck was very much in his mind; he wanted to see her. Find out what mischief she'd made in his absence. He tugged affably at the brim of his hat. "We start at dawn. I'll see you then."

Fletcher swallowed, nodded, then turned and rode away. Tristan headed in the opposite direction, driving those knot-headed cattle ahead of him, toward his own herd. The noon hour had come and gone by the time he'd ridden back to the house, splashed himself relatively clean, brushed his hair and put on a fresh shirt. He set out for the hills in a hurry he didn't want to consider too carefully, and found Emily there, with her sheep. She was sitting on a grassy knoll, watching them clip the grass to the roots, the dog resting beside her. Polymarr and Walter the mare were nowhere in sight.

"Still here?" he said, as though surprised. But he'd taken his hat off, and he was conscious that his hair was still damp from washing, and bore ridges from his comb.

The dog growled and sprang to his feet, and his dusty ruff stood out around his neck.

"Hush," Emily said, stroking the animal's head, and Spud made a whimpering sound and lay down again, muzzle on paws. Her attention turned, belatedly he thought, back to Tristan, and he felt a sweet sizzle somewhere behind his navel, just to look at her. "I live here," she told him, as though that settled all disagreement.

He sat down beside her, letting her remark

pass, and set his hat on the grass beside him. "This must be the sorriest way to make a living I've ever seen."

The corner of her mouth quivered, but she didn't smile. "I don't mind it," she said, after an interval of consideration. "It's an easy job."

Tristan rubbed his lower lip with the back of one hand. He sat cross-legged on the soft ground, enjoying the sweet, mingled scents of Miss Emily and the summer grass. "Yes, ma'am," he agreed, with a brief glance at Spud. "If a dog can do it, I reckon it is."

A slight flush climbed Emily's slender neck, and she wet her lips with the tip of her tongue, a gesture that was vengeance enough in its own right, if only she'd known it, but she didn't rise to the bait. "Spud," she said, "is a very smart animal."

He laughed, then looked around, squinting. "Where's Polymarr?"

"I sent him down to get his things out of the line shack. He's moving into the bunkhouse at the ranch."

"Is he, now? And here I told young Fletcher he'd have the place to himself."

Her flush deepened prettily and she cleared her throat in a delicate fashion. "I suppose it seems audacious, my hiring Mr. Polymarr away from you—" She fell silent, wretchedly embarrassed and, at the same time, determined to press for what she wanted.

Tristan was utterly charmed, though not ready to show it. "Listen, Miss Starbuck. If you want to live on the ranch and spoil whatever reputation you might have made for yourself, that's your business. Quite frankly, I would enjoy your company, but if you think I'm going to pack up and leave on your say-so, you are woefully mistaken."

"I could pay you something—some sort of compensation, I mean—after the shearing next spring."

Tristan barely refrained from rolling his eyes. "Even if I were willing to put up with those miserable sheep of yours—which I'm not—the other ranchers won't be. Once the word gets out that they're here, and that won't be long, believe me, the place will be under siege."

She blinked back tears, quickly, but not quickly enough. "We have to be somewhere," she said, evidently referring to herself and the sheep, and Tristan wanted to put his arms around her, though for the sake of her pride, he refrained. *"Somewhere,"* she repeated, so softly that she might have been talking to herself, or to God.

He ran his tongue along the inside of his lower lip. "You could sell the sheep," he said. "There must be somebody who'd want them." He knew he sounded doubtful, but there was no helping that. He wouldn't have given a beer token for the whole band.

She kept her head turned away, dabbed at one cheek with the edge of her grubby serape. "I'm not going to sell my flock," she said fiercely, when she'd recovered herself a little. Her eyes were puffy, but they flashed, and her nose, while reddened, was pitched at a stubborn angle. "If I have to fight to defend it, I will. It's all I have."

Mingled with the admiration he felt for this woman, and the very elemental attraction toward her, was a quiet annoyance. *"You'll* fight? One woman and an old man against half a dozen ranchers and their hired hands?" He thrust a hand through his hair. "I hope you don't plan on making a hell of a lot of headway, Miss Starbuck, because the two of you won't be much of a match for those outlaws."

"I'll do what I must to hold on to what's mine," she said.

He let out a ragged sigh. "Maybe you *want* to get yourself killed. Is that it? Life is just too hard and you're giving up?"

He'd been trying to exasperate her, but when she spoke, she sounded haughty as a duchess at high tea, which was amusing, in an irritating sort of way, her sitting there in men's pants and a serape that smelled pungently of sheep, acting fancy. "I assure you, my life is precious to me. If I was going to give up, it would have happened long before this."

The words intrigued him; he wondered, not for the first time, what sort of past lay behind her. Since he wasn't ready to talk about his own, however, he didn't raise the subject. Instead, he stood and dusted off his pants with both hands, then bent to retrieve his hat. In the process, he nearly bumped heads with Emily, and the desire to kiss her came over him with such sudden force that he felt unsteady.

She had fixed her attention on the .45. "Are you good with that?"

The question might have caught Tristan off-guard if he hadn't been paying attention. "Fair," he replied, and cleared his throat. He was not a shy man, not by any stretch of the imagination, but there was something about this woman that made him feel as awkward as a schoolboy in short pants.

"Have you ever killed anybody?"

He pretended not to hear. "I've got work to do," he said, moving toward the gelding. "I'll see you this evening." He mounted, tipped his hat and rode away.

Chapter

4

RETURNING TO THE BIG HOUSE that evening, after a long, dirty, hungry day, Emily felt her confidence slipping. Light glimmered through the windows of the kitchen, as she made her way toward the back door. After a moment's hesitation, during which she considered walking right in, regarding the property as her own the way she did, she knocked instead.

"In," commanded a good-natured voice, from the other side. From the place of light and warmth and belonging.

Emily entered, and found Tristan at the stove, cracking brown speckled eggs into a pan. He flashed one of his wounding grins at her. "I'm afraid this is all I know how to make," he said. "Never been much of a cook."

She hoped he hadn't heard the rumbling of her stomach and raised her chin. "I'm obliged," she said.

He gave her a look that seemed to take measure of her very soul, though there was nothing unseemly in it. "Are you?" he asked, his voice soft.

Why did she find this man's presence so soothing and, at one and the same time, so disturbing? He was fine-looking, yes, and he certainly had charm, but Emily had been practical all her life, and therefore not susceptible to such allure. Or so she'd thought.

She took a basin from its hook on the wall, carried it over to the stove. The eggs looked and smelled like ambrosia to her, though he'd nearly ruined them. "May I?" she said, indicating the water reservoir, with its chrome-handled lid.

"Be my guest," he said, removing their supper from the fire and setting it, skillet and all, in the center of the table.

Emily filled the basin and carried it outside, to the bench, where she found soap and a towel that smelled pleasantly of fresh air and Tristan. Hastily, she scrubbed her hands and face, fretted a moment over the sorry state of her hair, and went inside.

While other men would have gone ahead and begun the meal without her, Tristan had waited. He sat down only when she was seated, and nodded toward the strange mixture of over- and undercooked eggs.

She murmured her thanks and scooped out a healthy portion. It took all her willpower not to gobble the food, so ravenous was she, and she was halfway through when she realized Tristan wasn't eating.

"This stuff is terrible," he said, shoving his plate away.

Emily agreed, but she was starved, so she kept on, taking slow bites when she wanted to bury her face in the skillet, like Spud would do. "Yes," she said, refilling her plate. "Dreadful."

He laughed. "You are a woman of contradiction, Emily Starbuck," he told her.

The desperate hunger had finally begun to abate, and Emily laid down her fork at last, finished chewing, and swallowed, at a loss for a reply. She had been too busy surviving, of late, to ponder what sort of woman she was, and suddenly it was something she very much wanted to know.

Tristan got up and brought coffee to the table—coffee, that luxury she had gone without for so long—and set a cup in front of her.

"How," he began, in the same moderate tone as before, "did you manage to drive all those sheep from Montana to California by yourself?"

61

He was standing a few feet away by then, at the stove, the blue metal coffeepot in his hand, and his quiet regard was a great if inexplicable solace to Emily. She felt a peculiar need to take shelter in his arms, to rest her head against his shoulder, to share her hopes and secrets with him.

She stiffened, determined not to venture down a path that could only lead to degradation and heartbreak. Men like Tristan Saint-Laurent, handsome and prosperous, fitting easily into whatever place or circumstance in which they found themselves, merely dallied with women like her. And Emily did not intend to be dallied with.

"I didn't have a choice," she answered straightforwardly. She was tired to the core of her being, yearning for bath and bed, and yet there was an ember burning somewhere in her depths, a wanting for something else entirely. "I had inherited the sheep, and this land." She paused to let the latter part of the statement sink in. "I had nothing else, nowhere to go."

He studied her narrowly, standing next to the table with one foot braced against the bench, his own mug of coffee in hand. In anyone else, that would have been a breach of manners, but Tristan managed to look stately, and very much at ease. "You could have remarried."

She felt color sting her cheeks, looked away, then met his gaze again, fiercely proud. "I had one husband—that was enough."

"You must have been unhappy. I'm sorry."

"Don't be," she replied.

Tristan gave a low, exclamatory whistle. "I guess the poor bastard must have frozen to death," he said, after a few moments spent weighing the matter privately.

"It was not a love match," Emily said, her face still hot. She did not reach for her coffee, as her hands were trembling.

"All the same, you might be expected to at least *like* the man."

Emily did not look away, but neither did she reply. She had not felt anything for her late husband, except the devout hope that he would never, ever touch her. After his death, she had not even kept his name.

Tristan expelled a sigh. "All right, so you didn't even like him. Why in hell did you hitch yourself up to the man in the first place?"

There was within Emily a longing to know and be known, and for a brief interval that desire did ferocious battle with her pride. In the end, the former prevailed, a surprise in itself, for she had kept her spirit alive all these years by nurturing her dignity, that being pretty much all she had. "I needed a place to live. He needed someone to look after the house, after his first wife died."

Tristan was quiet for a long while, and when he spoke, there was no condemnation in his tone, no judgment. He was merely reflecting aloud, or so it seemed to Emily. "Why didn't you just hire on as a housekeeper?"

The question struck Emily like a slap, even

though she knew it wasn't hostile. "He would have had to pay me then," she said evenly. "Cyrus didn't spend any more money than he had to."

"You'd marry a man just to get a place to live?"

Emily rose, swept over to the cast-iron sink and set her plate inside. "I suppose I could have joined a brothel," she said, fully intending to shock him, and out of the corner of her eye she saw that she had succeeded, if the hardness of his jawline was any indication. She began scooping hot water from the reservoir to wash the dishes. "I was not trained to teach, and there were no fancy houses in our part of the country, where a maid might be wanted. So I married the first man who asked."

Tristan stepped into her path, stopping her fevered progress back and forth between the stove and the sink, taking the small bucket out of her hands and setting it aside with a thump. "I want to be the second," he said.

It was a good thing Emily wasn't holding the hot water any longer, because she would have dropped it and drenched them both. "What?"

"I need a wife. I think you'd do as well as anybody. You'd have a home and half-interest in this ranch. Our property dispute would be settled, too."

Emily stared up at him, stunned. Her first husband had been well past his virile years, God be thanked, but this one was young and vital, of an age to father children. He would make demands—intimate ones. "You can't be serious," she said, though some part of her hoped he was. "We're strangers. How do I know you're not a mean drunk, or even an outlaw?"

A tiny muscle in his cheek flexed, and Emily wondered distractedly if it was the word "outlaw" that had perturbed him. She saw a counterquestion take shape in his eyes, but with visible effort he quelled it, and spoke carefully. "I guess you'll just have to take me at my word," he said.

She raked her teeth over her lower lip. The offer, outlandish as it was, was not one she could afford to dismiss out of hand. While she felt certain that her claim on the ranch was just, she could not assume that a judge would agree. This was cattle country, after all, and Tristan had a foothold here. She had already experienced enough prejudice, because of the sheep, to know her position was a tenuous one, be it right or wrong, and while the injustice of that galled her sorely, she had to take it into consideration.

"What about my sheep?" she asked.

"Sell them. Tuck the money away someplace—I won't make any claim on it." He sounded so sure of himself and his ideas. What was it like, she wondered, to walk boldly through the world the way Tristan did, with that apparently innate sense of his own value, his right place in the scheme of things?

She balked. The sheep were all that she had, and much as she would have liked having a nest egg, the animals represented an asset with the propensity for renewing itself. Besides, whatever Tristan said now, as her husband, he could take the money away from her, with the full blessing of the courts. For that matter, he could sell, shoot or drive off every one of her sheep, with the same impunity. Once he put a golden band on her finger, she would have about as many rights as Spud did.

Still, the pull of home and husband, not to mention the prospect of a brood of children, was strong. She couldn't help picturing herself going to church of a Sunday, wearing a crisp frock and a fine bonnet, or chatting with the other women of the town at a quilting bee or an afternoon social. Her need for those things was almost as compelling as the beat of her heart and the steady flow of her breath. Almost.

"I don't even know you," she protested, full of sweet misery.

Tristan cupped her chin in his hand, raised it slightly, and looked deeply into her eyes. "This is who I am," he said, and then he bent his head and brushed her lips with his own. Gradually, the contact deepened, until it was forceful and, at the same time, heartbreakingly gentle.

Fire shot through her; she felt her knees wobble, and her heart threatened to fly away like a frightened bird, but she stepped into the kiss, instead of drawing back, as a more sensible woman might have done. When it ended, she swayed on her feet, utterly dazed, and to her profound embarrassment Tristan steadied her by taking her upper arms in his hands. His grin was wicked, insufferable and totally irresistible.

"Well?" he prompted. "Are we getting married or not?"

She flushed. "I suppose we could," she said.

His eyes laughed, and his mouth seemed to hover on the edge of another grin, but somehow he contrived to look—well—polite. "When?"

"There are so many things we haven't settled. The sheep—"

"Never mind the damn sheep. We'll deal with the problem somehow." He guided her to the table, sat her down, and straddled the bench beside her. His being so near affected her almost as much as the kiss had done. She touched her temple, feeling dizzy; then she drew a deep breath, expelled it. "There's something else. I have to know if you expect—if you will require—" Another breath, another exhalation. "Conjugal relations. Right away, I mean."

There was a tender quality to his smile, which made the mischief dancing in his eyes a little easier to forgive. "I'm not planning to fling you down in the tall grass the minute you say 'I do,' if that's what you mean."

How had this insane conversation begun? Emily began to rub both temples, and she was blushing furiously. "I will—would—need time. To get acquainted."

He grew pensive, considering his options no doubt, and then beamed another one of his grins at her. The impact nearly sent her spinning. "I want a real wife, Emily. But I'll give you a while to settle in."

"How long?" She could barely squeeze the words past her heart, which had lodged itself in her throat.

He made a magnanimous gesture with one hand. "Until I seduce you," he answered.

"Until you what?"

"Until I make you want to share my bed." There was that confidence again. That damnable certainty. "Fair enough?"

"You won't force me?"

He frowned. "I'll thank you not to insult me."

"You won't shoot my sheep?"

He raised a hand, like a man offering an oath. "Before God, I will not do those miserable creatures willful injury."

Emily wet her lips with the tip of her tongue, and the memory of Tristan's kiss pulsed in every nerve of her body, like an echo. "You'd better keep your promises," she warned, sustained by bravado and hope. "If you ever lay a hand on me or those sheep, I'll sew you up in the bedclothes while you're sleeping and beat you black and blue with a broom handle. And when those animals are sheared, come spring, and the wool and mutton has been sold, you'll be wise to leave my money be. If you try to steal it, you'd do well to take to the trail, because I'll shoot you for a thief if I catch up with you."

Tristan drew back in mock horror. "Those are mighty imaginative threats, Miss Emily. Methinks you either keep fast company or read too many dime novels."

Emily blushed again. In truth, she'd read about just such a stitching episode in a penny dreadful, and the image, vividly drawn, had stuck in her mind. "Nonetheless, I mean what I say."

"I believe you do." He put out his hand. "I will treat you as honorably as you treat me. Do we have a bargain?"

Emily could barely hear over the pounding of her pulses. She hesitated for a fraction of a moment, then placed her palm against his. It was like being struck by lightning, but she managed not to flinch. "We do," she said, and could not believe her own ears.

"You're doing what?" Shay demanded. He was mounted, while Tristan worked at mending another broken fence. The boy, Fletcher, who had arrived at dawn, with his bedroll, was using his gelding to round up the cattle for a head count.

Tristan knew his grin was the ingenuous, smart-ass reflection of Shay's own, and it pleased him to see his brother scowl in irritation. "I told you. I'm taking a wife. I figure we'll tie the knot on Sunday morning, after church."

Shay leaned down a little, his voice a harsh whisper, though no one was close enough to hear the exchange. "You don't know this woman from Adam's great-aunt!"

"I have an opinion or two where she's concerned," Tristan replied easily. He stroked the long neck of his brother's horse with a gloved hand.

"Do you love her?"

"I don't know," Tristan answered. "I think I could."

"Suppose you're wrong?"

"Suppose I'm right? I want what you have, Shay. You ought to understand that better than anybody."

The mirror image softened a little. "I hope this isn't a mistake," Shay said.

"Believe me, so do I. Now. What brings you out here on this fine day?"

Shay swept his hat off and resettled it. "Two things," he replied. "I got a wire from the warden at the state penitentiary today, saying Kyle took sick last month and died two days ago. If you want to buy the Powder Creek spread, you ought to talk to his lawyer, Tom Rutledge."

"And the other thing?" Tristan prompted, when the silence had stretched on for a while.

"It's those sheep of Miss Emily's. Word's gotten around that they're here, and there's some fretting among the ranchers. Folks want to drive them out before they ruin the grazing land."

Although Tristan himself had no particular fondness for sheep, and although he wasn't the least bit surprised, had even predicted the problem, the bald-faced presumption of it got his back up. "They needn't vex themselves," he said, with a calmness that was only partly genuine. "It's my grass those bleating woollies are cropping off at the dirt. My cattle that could go hungry."

Shay leaned forward, bracing one arm on the pommel of his saddle, and sighed. "You know damn well it isn't that simple," he said. "The reasoning goes that if they let in one sheep farmer, there'll soon be a plague of them. There's been some pretty crazy talk already, and while most of those windbags are just jawing, a few of them have fallen on hard times lately, and they sound real bitter. You're going to have trouble if you don't get that flock back on the trail, pronto."

Nothing would have pleased him more, but if the sheep went, Miss Emily Starbuck would surely go with them. He could not, would not, let that happen. Furthermore, he'd given his word that the greasy beasts would meet with no ill fortune while in his keeping, which pretty much meant he had to look after them as if they were as good as cattle.

"I appreciate the warning. How's Aislinn? That baby on the way yet?"

Shay paled at the mention of the impending birth, though the light of joy and pride shone in his eyes. "Time's getting close," he said. "She stayed home from the store this morning to sit in the parlor with a pillow plumped behind her back."

For the ambitious Aislinn, that was unusual behavior indeed. "You send word when it happens. I've never been an uncle before."

Shay swallowed. "I've never been a father. As far as I know, anyway."

"You'll do just fine," Tristan answered. For him, that was sloppy sentiment.

"You look out for yourself, and that woman of yours," Shay said, reining his horse away. A moment later, he was riding back toward town.

Tristan went back to his work, but his mind was elsewhere.

The sheep were quiet, enjoying the sweet grass and the plenitude of water flowing from the spring, and the scene was so pastoral that Emily, keeping watch on the hillside, let down her guard and drifted off to sleep. Mr. Polymarr was somewhere far afield, hunting rabbits for supper, so it was Spud that warned her of the approaching riders. If it hadn't been for him, they might have trampled her, streaming over the knoll behind her the way they did.

She was on her feet in a trice, the aged .38 shaking in her hand and aimed for the middle of the lead man's chest. The sheep, startled, began to mill and cry, and Emily spoke quietly to the dog. "Keep them together, boy."

Spud was reluctant to leave her side, but at her command he darted off to drive the splintering sheep back into the band. There were six riders, and though the brands on the flanks of their horses were varied ones, Emily supposed they'd come from the Powder Creek place.

"What do you want?" she asked, squaring her shoulders.

The desperadoes were tremendously pleased with themselves. "We came to relieve you of them sheep, ma'am," said one. He carried a shotgun, as did several of his companions, and Emily knew she would be cut down if there was gunplay. She could probably plug the leader easily enough, but in the next moment, she'd be dead, too.

She raised the pistol, extending her arm to its full length, amazed at how steady her grip had become, when her palm was slippery with sweat, and thumbed back the hammer. *Please,* she prayed simultaneously, *don't let this thing go off.* "You men just turn around and ride out of here," she said, "and everything will be all right."

They looked at each other, amused and quite undaunted. Between them, they could wipe out her flock, leave the sheep to rot; she'd heard of such things happening. She planted her feet and held her ground.

"You can't protect these pitiful critters, ma'am," said the spokesman, with a courtly touch to his hat brim, "if you'll pardon my sayin' so. Not by yourself, leastways."

It was then that a bullet struck the ground just a foot or so in front of his horse. The animal shrieked and skittered backward, rolling its eyes and tossing its head. Emily turned, expecting to see Tristan sighting in for another shot, but to her disappointment and relief, it was Mr. Polymarr and the boy, Fletcher.

"Ride out," Polymarr said. He looked like Methuselah's grandfather, but he was sprightly with a weapon, and you could tell by his stance and his tone that he meant business.

" 'Tween the three of us, we can get every damn one of you 'fore you so much as wheel them horses towards home."

One of the men drew, partly hidden from Mr. Polymarr's view by the other riders, and before her next heartbeat, Emily had fired. By luck, rather than skill, the shot nicked the assailant's right wrist and sent his pistol clattering to the ground.

At that, someone cursed, and Emily watched with disbelief as the barrel of a rifle swung toward her, shining nickel glinting in the cool afternoon sunlight. It seemed to move slowly, as though the air had turned to water, but even before she could pitch herself to the ground, there was a second blast, and her would-be killer flew backward out of the saddle.

"I told you I'd shoot," Mr. Polymarr said, and spat.

The sheep were in a state of pandemonium by then, and Spud was barking wildly, frantically, torn between defending his mistress and keeping the flock together. In the end, he stayed with his terrified charges.

After recovering their fallen comrade, the riders turned and fled. Emily, watching them, had no doubt whatsoever that they would return. They'd just be more devious about it the next time, that was all. Bullies, every one of them. And cowards, too.

Mr. Polymarr and the boy rushed toward her, swung down off the ancient horses Tristan used to pull his buckboard.

"You all right, miss?" Fletcher demanded.

His freckles seemed to stand out an inch from his face, but it was the gentle bleakness in his eyes that moved Emily. Young as he was, he'd experienced suffering firsthand; she could tell that just by looking at him.

"Yes," she said. She wanted to reassure the boy somehow, but his physical attitude did not invite familiarity. "Yes, I'm fine." She caught Mr. Polymarr up in her gaze. "I'm grateful to you both."

Fletcher was pale, though his freckles had settled back into place. He glanced nervously in the direction the riders had taken. "Those were Powder Creek men. They'll be back for certain."

Polymarr nodded, his knuckles going white with the strength of his grasp on the rifle he carried. He was red and sweating profusely, and his breathing was shallow and raspy, but Emily knew better than to inquire after his well-being. He would not appreciate special concern. "It's started, then." He turned his head and met Emily's eyes. "This here, miss, is just the beginnin'."

A weight of sorrow descended upon Emily, momentarily crushing her. She struggled to hold on to her dream. "They were no better than outlaws. Good men don't enforce their will with guns." But even as she spoke the words, she was recalling the ranchers all along the trail from Montana, taking grim care that she didn't settle in their territory. They'd been law-abiding men, husbands and fathers, brothers and sons, but they'd plainly viewed the sheep, and Emily herself, as a threat. For her, the open range had been closed tight.

"We've gotta move these critters down-hill," Polymarr announced, rubbing his stubbly chin. "Closer to the house and barn."

"I don't work with no sheep," Fletcher said.

Emily ignored him. "Tristan won't like that," she pointed out to Mr. Polymarr.

"Well, I don't reckon he will," the old man agreed. "But if you want to keep these animals alive till spring, you've got to do somethin'." He gestured toward Powder Creek. "Once it gets dark, miss, those fellers will be back, and they'll bring their friends and relations. These here sheep will be easy pickin's then, and it will be next to impossible to protect them, there bein' no place to dig in for a fight."

Before Emily could respond, Spud took to barking again, and she was braced for battle when Tristan came riding out of the brush. She was so startled that she nearly shot him out of pure reflex.

"What the hell happened here?" he demanded, swinging down off the gelding's glistening back before it had come to a stop. Clearly, he had heard the shots, probably at some distance, and made haste to discover their source.

"We've had ourselves a social call from the Powder Creek crew, that's all," Mr. Polymarr replied, with some relish and another stream of spittle. "Shot two of 'em—I got one, and the lady here got the other."

"Sweet God," Tristan breathed. It was the first time she had seen him falter, but then, she'd only known him one day, for all that he'd proposed marriage and she'd agreed. Then his jawline hardened and he took an ominous step in Emily's direction. "Are you willing to get yourself killed for these damned sheep?"

She didn't retreat, although she was secretly intimidated. "Yes," she said. "They are every bit as important to me as your cattle are to you."

He yanked off his hat and slapped his thigh with it in exasperation, and in a sidelong glance, Emily saw both Mr. Polymarr and Fletcher move back, out of range. Tristan's hair gleamed like so much spun gold, for all that it was mussed and dusty. "Damnation," he growled, "but you are a foolish woman!"

"I want to protect what's mine. Just like you."

He closed his eyes briefly, thrust a hand through his hair. His struggle for patience was obvious. "It was bad enough that you brought sheep into cattle country. God only knows what will happen now."

"A range war, that's what," put in Polymarr, from a judicious distance.

"Are you saying I should have stood by and watched while they scattered or even killed my flock?"

"Of course not!"

"Then what should I have done? What would *you* have done?"

He opened his mouth to speak, closed it again without uttering another word. He simply whirled away from her, strode to his horse and mounted.

"What about these sheep?" Polymarr wanted to know, looking from Emily to Tristan and back again. "We might just as well plug 'em our own selves as leave 'em here."

"Put them in the lower pasture," Tristan snapped. His gaze was hot enough to warp hardwood. "I'll deal with the visitors."

Emily sprang forward, before he could ride away, and grasped the gelding's bridle. "No," she said. She swallowed, and her pride went down, but not easily, and not without pain. "Please, Tristan. They'll kill you."

Polymarr and Fletcher had begun to argue about moving the sheep, while Spud trotted tirelessly back and forth along the outer edges of the flock.

Tristan's eyes were like blue flint. "There's a good chance of that," he replied. "But nobody—*nobody* rides onto my land and makes threats."

She laid a hand to his thigh, felt the muscles go taut beneath fabric and flesh. "Don't go alone. Ride to town and fetch your brother first. Please."

"No."

"He's the marshal—it's his job to settle disputes like this—"

"He has a wife, a baby on the way. Aislinn's brothers and Miss Dorrie, they all depend on him. I won't put him in danger."

"Then take me with you."

He glowered down at her for a long moment.

"Go look after your sheep, Little Bo Peep,"
he said, with quiet bitterness. Then, as she
watched in misery and fear, he rode off,
headed toward Powder Creek.

Chapter

5

TRISTAN HADN'T GOTTEN FAR when the gelding
came up lame. Maybe it was Providence,
maybe it was just plain sorry luck, but there
was nothing he could do, for the moment, but
turn back. He'd pay his respects at Powder
Creek another time, and make a point of
doing it soon.

Carefully, he pried a stone out of the animal's
hoof, but the soft flesh was bruised. On foot,
with the horse limping along behind him, he
set himself toward home. Of necessity, he
made slow progress, but not so slow that he
didn't catch up with that squalling mob of
sheep. The gelding turned skittish at the
noise and the smell, and it took some doing
to calm him down.

He and Emily exchanged a look as he came
alongside the flock, but neither made any

attempt to speak. It would have been futile anyhow, with all that fuss-and-fidget going on.

A gentleman, he reflected, would help drive the stupid creatures to their new pasture, but that day he wasn't feeling very gracious. He'd asked the woman to marry him—he still wanted her more than he could admit, even to himself—but since then he'd begun to question his sanity.

Oh, plenty of hasty weddings took place, especially out West, where women, handsome ones in particular, were at a premium, and babies had a way of coming ahead of schedule, but Tristan had always envisioned a different scenario for himself. He'd planned on abstaining from private pleasures, once he'd chosen a bride, and courting her properly, though with dispatch, wooing her with flowers and pretty words, bedding her only when she was his lawful wife. The first child, he'd always figured, would come after a full nine months had passed, that there should be no scandal attached to the boy's name—he wanted a son first, so there'd be someone to look after his daughters when he wasn't around.

Now, here was Emily, and abstaining was the last thing he wanted to do. It seemed plainly impossible, and after all, they would be standing up before a preacher come Sunday.

Reaching the barn, he took the gelding inside, took up a pitchfork to muck out a stall and put down fresh straw. That done, he cleaned the wounded hoof and treated it with salve. Meanwhile, Emily, Polymarr, the dog and the boy—who had turned sullen but was helping nonetheless—were herding the sheep into his best pasture to graze right alongside his cattle. Shaking his head, he muttered a curse and strode toward the house.

He'd clean up, he decided, and when Fletcher and the old man got through playing sheepherder, he'd take one of the old plow horses they were riding and go to town. For one thing, he needed more horses, and more men, if he was going to run the operation right. And it had occurred to him, during the long walk down the hill, that there was another way to handle his grievance with the raiders from Powder Creek. He could buy the place, and send the lot of them packing.

Meeting the price, undoubtedly high, wouldn't be a problem; he had plenty of cash, thanks to the wise investment he'd made a few years before, in his own stagecoach line, since sold at a hefty profit. He preferred not to ruminate too much on where the seed money had come from; those days had dissipated into nothing, like thin smoke, and he had no desire to resurrect them in memory.

He was smiling as he filled a couple of buckets with hot water from the stove reservoir and carried them outside to the bench, where he liked to wash, since he always indulged in considerable splashing. He stripped off his shirt, hung it on a wooden peg, and reached for the soap. He was all lathered up when Emily startled him halfway out of his hide by sneaking up on him from behind.

He swore again, though more moderately than he might have done in other company.

"I am glad to see that you've come to your senses," she said. "Those men might well have killed you."

Tristan poured a bucket of water over himself, to rinse off the soap suds, road grit and sweat. "I'd be there now," he said pointedly, "if my horse hadn't picked up a rock." Her color flared a little at the challenge; he loved it when that happened—seeing it was like laying down a high straight in a game of cards.

"Then you're a fool," she said.

"I won't argue that." He reached for the other bucket and doused himself a second time. His trousers were wet through, and he was hard, and there was no hiding it. He wasn't sure he even *wanted* to hide it. "I'll speak to the preacher while I'm in Prominence. Unless you've changed your mind, that is."

She looked away, looked back. "I haven't changed my mind," she said, pinkening up again, real bright. Blessed God, she was stubborn, and he loved that, too.

He extended one arm to brace himself against the sidewall of the kitchen, deliberately capturing her gaze and holding it, just to prove that he could. "Listen to me," he said, and for all his easy stance, he was deadly serious. "If anybody comes looking for trouble, you leave those sheep to their fate and hightail it for the house. You might be foolish enough to die for a lot of mutton stew and woolen underwear, but that's too much to ask of Fletcher and the old fellow. Do I make myself clear?"

She swallowed, nodded. It made him mad that she didn't seem to place as much value on her own safety as that of two virtual strangers.

He kissed her forehead, just lightly. "I'll be back as soon as I can. Is there anything you want from the general store?"

She scrounged up a dusty smile. "Something for supper—besides eggs. Mr. Polymarr went rabbit hunting this morning, before those outlaws came along, but he didn't have much luck."

"I'd say he had more than his share of good fortune, just getting out of there alive. So did you. Be careful, Emily. I mean it."

She nodded, and he headed into the house, mounted the stairs to his bedroom and put on dry pants and a clean shirt. After combing out his wet hair, he went outside again, and found Fletcher waiting with the nag he'd been riding all day. He was leading Polymarr's horse by the reins.

"I thought maybe you'd want some company," the boy said.

Tristan was touched, though of course he took proper care not to show it and embarrass the kid. "You'd best stay here," he said brusquely, taking the reins of the second horse and climbing into the saddle. "Look after Miss Emily and the old man."

Fletcher gulped down a protest, then gave a glum nod. "You're going to need a hell of a lot more men than just me and Polymarr if you mean to keep those sheep from being slaughtered," he observed. "And it'll be hard getting help, cattle-folk being like they are."

"You're right about that," Tristan admitted, with a sigh of resignation. "But I'm going to get the hands I need, that much is certain. Sweep out the bunkhouse, because I plan to bring home some company."

He asked himself, as he rode toward Prominence at the best pace the horse could manage, which wasn't impressive, why he'd ever let himself get knotted up in this predicament with Emily in the first place. He was a cattleman himself, and thus he sympathized with the ranchers' position. He had no use for sheep, except in the form of good, serviceable wool. Still, the answer wasn't hard to calculate: one look at Emily Starbuck, in her ragbag serape and slouch hat, and he'd lost every ounce of good sense he'd ever had.

Emily owned one dress, a blue calico, and it was rolled up and stuffed into the bottom of the small leather kit bag that held the few possessions she'd collected over the years—an old tortoiseshell hairbrush with bent bristles, a frayed camisole and a pair of drawers of butternut linen, and a copy of a dime novel about a handsome outlaw and a fancy Eastern lady. There were pages missing now, but that was all right; she'd read through it so many times that she could have recited the story without once referring to the print between its tattered covers. She particularly liked the part where the heroine sewed the villain into his own bedsheets and pounded him like berry pulp in a flour-sack dish towel.

When Spud, Mr. Polymarr and Fletcher had gotten the sheep to settle down, and she'd scanned every horizon for another batch of raiders, Emily went inside, built up the fire in the cookstove, and commenced pumping water to refill the near-empty reservoir. While it was heating, she shook out the tattered frock and hunted down a round copper washtub. By the time she'd carried that upstairs, into one of the spare rooms, purloined soap, a washcloth and a towel from the wash-stand in Tristan's bedroom, and carried half a dozen buckets to the tub, a precious hour had passed.

After propping a chair under the latch of the spare-room door, she stripped to the skin, stepped into the shallow but still-steaming water and sank down into it with a sigh of well-earned contentment. There was no time for lounging—Tristan might come back at any moment—but that didn't matter. It was luxury enough, just to be clean.

Later, clad in the calico, she half carried, half dragged the tub down the stairs and out-side, through the kitchen, to empty it off the side of the stoop. She rinsed the receptacle and returned it to its place in one of the sheds, then went back up to the spare room to brush her hair and wind it into a braid. After a glimpse into Tristan's shaving mirror—although she had slept in that room the night before, she had not been comfortable with the idea of bathing there—she pronounced herself presentable and returned to the kitchen.

A thorough search of shelves, bins and cupboards yielded the makings for baking soda biscuits, and she was rolling the dough out on the freshly scrubbed table when Fletcher rapped lightly at the open door. "Ma'am?"

She smiled at him, but some of her good cheer faded when she remembered the sheep and the men from Powder Creek, who were probably plotting revenge at that moment, if they hadn't already settled on a plan. "Is everything all right?"

"Yes, ma'am," Fletcher said, and even in that short stretch of words, his voice broke a couple of times. He was even younger, Emily realized, than she'd thought. "Polymarr, he sent me to see that you were safe." He took in her dress and tidy hair. "You sure do look different. I would hardly have knowed you."

She suppressed a second smile, but he turned red anyway. "Thank you," she said. "I think."

Fletcher remembered his hat with a painfully obvious jolt, and snatched it off his head. "I was making a compliment, right enough," he said, his Adam's apple bobbing.

Emily made a point of looking away for one merciful moment. "You're very kind," she told him softly. "I'll bring you some supper, when it's ready." She didn't qualify the promise, but it did depend on Tristan's timely return and his good memory. Given the perils they all faced, though, she'd be happy if he merely came back, with or without supplies.

The sun had set and the lamps were lit when she heard a commotion outside, snatched up the .38 and hurried to investigate.

Tristan had arrived, with eight stout horses, each one ridden by an Indian. Grinning, he loosed a burlap bundle tied behind his saddle and handed it down to her. "There're two chickens in there, along with some other things." He cocked his thumb. "You don't need to fix for the new sheepherders—they prefer their own cooking."

Emily held the bundle of goods tightly, almost overcome with relief, not because there would be fried chicken for supper, but because there were no holes in Tristan. Because he was home, safe and sound. "Is there news of Aislinn?" she asked, after her heartbeat had played leapfrog with itself for a few long seconds.

Again, the grin flashed, brilliantly white in the thickening twilight. "The doctor's with her now."

"Is she well?"

He got down from the saddle, spoke briefly to one of the Indians, who nodded in reply, and turned back to her. "She's in better shape than Shay is," he replied. "If I didn't know for certain I'm his twin, I'd think he was beside himself."

Suddenly it seemed too personal, their discussing the coming of the McQuillans' child, out in the open and in plain hearing of eight Indians. Sparing Tristan only a nod, she lowered her eyes, spun around, and fled into the house.

She opened the parcel on the table, and found the chickens inside, plucked and dressed, along with a tin of lard, some yeast and spices, a packet of tea, a dozen potatoes, several tins of green beans and four dime novels, carefully wrapped in butcher paper and tied with string. Her eyes filled with tears, just to suppose, for the briefest interval of time, that they might be intended for her. She couldn't remember the last time she had received an actual gift, although she was not ungrateful for her inheritance, uncertain as it was.

Try though she did to imagine Tristan immersed in stories bearing titles like *Vivian and the Sultan* and *The Loyal and Tender Heart,* quite without success, it was simply too reckless to hope for such a present. He owned a number of books, and she had already examined those, running her hands over the fine leather bindings in reverence and envy. He seemed to prefer history, mathematics and classic literature.

She busied herself with the making of supper, and when the meal was ready, she went to the door and called to Tristan. It was a bittersweet pleasure, doing that homey thing— sweet because she could pretend to be part of a family, and bitter for precisely the same reason: it was merely pretense.

Tristan washed up outside, and when he came back, Mr. Polymarr and Fletcher were with him, hats in hand, faces red from scrubbing, probably with cold water pumped from the well. Emily, who had been filling two plates to take out to them, smiled and made places for the men at the table instead.

It was a feast, that meal, made up of crisply fried chicken, potatoes and biscuits, thick gravy and green beans. For a long time, the men ate in silent earnest, made hungry by their hard work, and Emily took pleased satisfaction in their enjoyment, for she was a proud cook, and it had been a long while since she'd had the makings of so fine a dinner.

Presently, Mr. Polymarr wiped his mouth on the sleeve of his shirt, helped himself to the last biscuit, and warned Tristan, "You'd better watch them Injuns real close. They got a long, cold winter comin' on, and a lot of mouths to feed. Could be them sheep'll look mighty good to them."

Tristan met Emily's gaze, and she saw a teasing smile lurking in his eyes. "I can always hope," he said.

She thought of how she'd be married to this man, come Sunday, of how they'd live alone together in this house, sharing meals and plans and problems. Eventually, they would share a bed, too, of course. She felt shy, all of a sudden, and got up to clear the table.

In a moment, Tristan was beside her, holding his own empty plate. He'd done credit to the meal, though he hadn't eaten as much as either of their hired men. "Leave this for me to do," he said.

Emily had never known a man to wash dishes before, never even heard of one doing so, but of course he must have done. He'd been living alone, at least for a while, and the whole place was tidy.

"Go on in there and sit by the fire a while," he said, nodding to indicate the stone hearth at the other end of the house. He set his plate and Emily's in the sink, then retrieved the dime novels from the sideboard, where she'd put them earlier, to keep them out of harm's way. "The storekeeper—her name's Dorrie McQuillan— said these just came in last week, on the stage from Sacramento." With that, he put them in her hands.

She stared at them, her throat tight with an indefinable emotion.

He tapped at the books with an index finger, and there was a note of gentle amusement in his voice. "I'd like to read the one about the servant girl who becomes a trick rider in a Wild West show and then marries a count. That's quite a range of experience."

Emily met his gaze, and only when it was too late did she realize there were tears standing in her eyes. "I don't know what to say. Besides—besides thank you."

He set her back on her heels with that wicked flash of a grin. " 'Thank you' will do," he told her. Then he collected the plates

Fletcher and Polymarr had left behind—at some point they had both fled the kitchen without her noticing—and put those in the sink, too. "I'd better go out there and make sure the new men are comfortable."

She merely nodded, since no reply came to mind that wouldn't sound foolish. She was glad he'd referred to the Indians as "the new men," instead of using some cruder term, as Mr. Polymarr had done.

Tristan touched her face with the backs of his fingers, then gave her braid a light pull that tugged at something far deeper and more mysterious. "You look real pretty," he said, and the simple words, spoken in a soft, hoarse tone, had the effect of an accolade.

Emily bit her lower lip. She might have been draped in velvet and dripping diamonds, instead of a hand-me-down calico frock, the way he made her feel, and while she reminded herself that he was a charmer, very clever with words, it didn't do much good.

Just when she thought she would succumb and throw her arms around his neck, he turned and left her standing there, in front of the sink, with the dime novels in her hands. She didn't stir for some time.

The Indians, splinters from a number of fractured tribes, had set up camp at the edge of the pasture. They had a good fire going, and the aroma of roasting meat mingled with the scents of smoke and grass and sheep. If they were having mutton for dinner, Tristan reasoned, that was fine with him.

The dog fell in beside him, gave a friendly yelp, and licked the heel of his palm. Tristan greeted the animal with a quiet word and a pat on the head.

Polymarr appeared out of the gloom, carrying the shotgun he was rarely without. It was sobering, the image of this crotchety old man wandering around in the dark with a loaded gun. Next to that, the prospect of entertaining a bunch of angry riders from Powder Creek seemed downright agreeable. "Them damn savages is cookin' up a dog or somethin'," he muttered.

"Never mind the supper menu," Tristan replied, irritated. "Have they posted guards around the sheep?"

Grudgingly, Polymarr nodded. "Fact is, there ain't much for me and the boy to do."

"You've earned yourself a rest anyway. Why don't you head for the bunkhouse and get some sleep."

"And risk gettin' my hair lifted?"

Tristan laughed. "Not much of a risk," he said, "since you don't *have* any hair to speak of."

Fletcher joined the party. He wouldn't meet Tristan's eyes; not surprising, given the way he'd looked at Emily during supper. Tristan couldn't blame him; she had been a sight to fasten on.

"You think it's smart, lettin' those Injuns have guns?" the boy asked.

"They'd have a hell of a time fighting off any night visitors without them," Tristan answered. "Just mind your business, and let them tend to theirs, and things will be fine."

Polymarr looked skeptical, and gave a great sigh. "I reckon I *am* a mite on the weary side. You sure I ain't gonna get my throat cut while I'm sleepin'?"

"I guess that depends on whether you snore or not," Tristan answered, and went on, the dog accompanying him, while the other two men headed for the bunkhouse. He walked the perimeter of the flock, found sentries in their proper places and returned to the house, where his thoughts had been all along.

Inside, he filled the sink with hot water and washed up the dishes, but all the while he was watching Emily, at the edge of his vision, sitting next to the fireplace, absorbed in one of the books he'd bought for her. He thought it ironic that she found the lives of fictional characters so fascinating, when her own included a fair amount of adventure. How many women could drive a flock of sheep all the way from Montana to California, with only a dog to help and protect them? How many could face down a pack of gun-toting thieves the way she had, that very day, up in the hills?

He shook his head, bemused. It seemed to him that Emily Starbuck ought to be writing those books, instead of just reading them.

Twenty minutes later, when he joined her at the other end of the house, she looked up from the pages at last, eyes wide and luminous.

"How did you know she was going to become a trick rider and marry a count?" she asked, in a breathless way that set something to quivering inside him.

For a moment or two, he was confounded as to what she might be talking about. Confounded about a few other things, too, come to think about it. But then it struck him that she was referring to the plot of the dime novel. "I skimmed it while Dorrie was filling my order. She'll be bringing some other supplies out tomorrow, by the way."

Her eyes went wider still. "You read it?" She glanced at the shelves of leather-bound volumes he cherished. "This?"

"Sure. A book's a book. I like them all. That one has a bang-up ending."

Suddenly she laughed. It was a soft, musical sound, wholly feminine, and it roused an uncharacteristic shyness in him, an aspect of his nature that he had not recognized before. The sound of an approaching rider saved him; he found that his usually glib tongue was tangled, and the visitor gave him an excuse to leave the house.

Strapping on his .45 with hasty, practiced motions, he wondered if his neck had gone red. The identity and intentions of the rider were lesser concerns, which only went to prove that the right woman could set a man's brain to rattling around his head like a peach pit in a tin can.

Fortunately, when he went outside, he found Shay there, glowing like he'd swallowed the moon whole. "It's a girl," he said jubilantly, as he jumped down from the gelding.

Tristan responded with a happy exclamation and a slap on the shoulder. Then, more seriously, he asked, "How's Aislinn?"

Shay's face softened at the mention of the wife he adored. "She's the most incredible woman," he said, and from his reverent tone, one might have drawn the conclusion that nobody else had ever borne a child before. "Hell, I'd rather let a blind man dig a bullet out of me with a butter knife than go through what she did. But there she is, sitting up in bed, holding the baby and looking pretty as an angel. To see her now, you'd think she never broke a sweat."

Tristan smiled. "I'd offer you a drink in celebration, but you'd probably rather get back."

Shay glanced toward the house, and from his expression, Tristan knew Emily was standing in the doorway. He glanced back, saw her framed in an aura of soft light, and thought to himself that Aislinn wasn't the only one with the look of an angel about her.

"Things are a little tense in town," Shay admitted, lowering his voice. "Tristan, the ranchers aren't happy about those sheep. Some of them say you've sold them out."

He folded his arms. "I can't much help what they think," he said evenly. Then he grinned. "When can I have a look at this little girl of yours? And what's her name going to be?"

"You're welcome anytime," Shay said, as though surprised by the question. "Aislinn wants to christen her Mattie."

Mattie. The name of the young woman who had given birth to them only hours after being widowed in an Indian attack and then dying herself. "That's a fine choice," he said, and cleared his throat.

Shay was preparing to mount up again. He nodded toward Emily. "Come and see us as soon as you can." The vaguest suggestion of a grin touched his mouth. "Bring your friend."

Tristan promised to visit, asked his brother to convey his congratulations to Aislinn, and watched as Shay disappeared into the night. He felt a pang of fear, looking after him, and hoped that badge he prized so much wouldn't get him killed.

"The baby's arrived?" Emily asked, when he was inside the house again, his earlier embarrassed bewilderment forgotten.

He nodded. "A girl. They're going to call her Mattie." He went to the pine cupboard beside the fireplace, took out a bottle and a glass, and poured himself a whiskey to mark the occasion. "I'm an uncle."

Emily watched as he raised the glass to his lips and took a sip, but because of the shadows he couldn't make out her expression. "You're worried," she said. "Why?"

He couldn't tell her that he was afraid his brother might get caught in the range war that was almost sure to come about because of those blasted sheep. It wouldn't have been fair to lay such a burden on her, even if she had brought the flock to Prominence. Whatever his own feelings about the stupid critters might be, she obviously valued them, and she had that right.

In the end, he told her part of the truth. "There's some mean talk in town," he said, after another sip of whiskey. "The boys from Powder Creek aren't the only ones, Bo Peep, who find your sheep objectionable."

She turned her face toward the fire, and he saw in its glow that her cheeks were bright with indignation. The dime novel lay in her lap. "What do they expect me to do?"

"Move on," he replied.

Her gaze sliced to his. "Is that what you want?"

He considered the question, though he'd long since made his decision. "No," he said, "but I could do without the sheep."

She sighed, one finger curved to mark her place in the book. Once again, she was staring into the crackling fire, and its light danced along the length of her shining hair. Tristan wanted to touch her, but he restrained himself. Sunday—their wedding day—was not far off. That night, when she was officially his wife, he would begin his campaign to bed her, but he would be patient, whatever the cost. His honor depended upon that.

"Is it true that cattle and sheep cannot coexist?" she asked, after a long time. Her voice was small and fragile, but he knew that she was one of the strongest people he had ever encountered.

"No," he said, with weary resignation. "If a man's got plenty of range land, he can move the flock from one pasture to another, so the grass has time to grow back. It isn't the animals that can't get along, Emily. It's their owners."

She stood, slowly, proudly, elegantly. "That flock is all I have," she said.

He wanted to tell her that wasn't so, that he meant to give her the world, but it wasn't the time for encouraging speeches, so he kept his mouth shut.

"You'll be sleeping in the barn again?" she asked, when he didn't speak right away.

He thrust out a hard sigh. "Yup," he said, and finished his whiskey in one gulp.

Chapter

6

THE WEDDING BAND GLEAMED in the lamplight of the barn, a small golden circle in the palm of his hand. Tristan closed his fingers around it for an instant, as though it were a talisman, and then shoved it back into the pocket of his pants. Trying to calculate how long it would take, after the wedding on Sunday, to have his way with Emily, he put out the light, lay down in the hayloft and made up his mind to sleep.

Instead, he imagined Emily giving birth to their child, sometime in the not-too-distant future. He knew she'd be brave, as Aislinn had been, but he expected his own reaction would be similar to Shay's. Stoic as he might appear on the surface, inside, he'd be in a frenzy.

Mentally, he worked his way backward from that momentous day, and inevitably came to the time of conception. The pictures were so vivid that he groaned. He was in a bad way, and feared he would not soon see an improvement in his situation. The hell of it was that his personal code would not allow him to find his ease elsewhere; from the moment Emily had promised herself to him, he'd been committed.

He spent the next hour or so tossing and turning, but the day had been a long and difficult one, and he was tired, so presently he lapsed into a shallow, fitful sleep. The sound of the dog whining at the base of the ladder awakened him, some time later, and he raised himself onto one elbow.

"What?" he snapped, and started down the ladder.

Spud whimpered, and there was an all-too-familiar coppery smell, mingling with the usual ones of hay and horse manure and sweaty animal hide. Blood.

Tristan felt his way to the lamp that hung from one of the low beams, struck a match, and lit the wick. The dog looked up at him with doleful eyes, and whined again, apologetically. Squatting in the straw, Tristan examined the animal and found he'd been torn up pretty badly in a fight of some sort. Probably, he'd tangled with a raccoon or a badger, maybe even a bobcat, prowling around waiting to make a swipe at the sheep, but one thing was definite: he'd come up the loser.

As gently as possible, Tristan lifted the dog in both arms and headed for the house. The Indians keeping watch were shadowy forms in the darkness, and their campfire blazed a bright warning to all intruders, whether they had two legs or four. Spud must have wandered a fair distance from the flock, a strange thing in and of itself.

Inside, he set the dog in the center of the kitchen table and started lighting lamps. Spud made sorrowful complaint, and the sound must have awakened Emily, for she appeared while Tristan was filling a basin from the hot water reservoir. Not that he'd tried to be all that quiet.

Seeing the dog's blood-matted fur, she gasped and went white. She was wearing one of his shirts for a nightgown, and he tried not to notice that her legs were showing. And fine legs they were, too.

"What happened?" she cried, rushing over to stroke the animal's head with a loving hand. For all that something had practically shredded the poor creature's hide, Tristan envied him a little, just then, wanting that tenderness for himself.

He got liniment and a clean cloth from the shelf where he kept such supplies, accidents being a fairly common occurrence on a ranch. In the past, though, he'd only had himself for a patient. He dampened the cloth with pungent medicine and began to clean the worst of the dog's wounds, a six-inch gash on his left flank.

Spud showed his teeth and growled, no doubt prompted by the pain, but Emily spoke to him with a sort of stern compassion, and he quieted down a little. Tristan figured he might have been short a finger or two by then, if it hadn't been for her.

"Will he die?" she asked, when the job was nearly finished, and Tristan realized that she'd been working up her courage to pose the question all along.

"Probably not," he answered. "He won't be much use with the sheep for a while, though. These wounds are sure to get infected if he doesn't stay clean until they've closed up."

Emily shut her eyes and rested her forehead against the crown of the dog's head for a moment, and Spud made a low sound in his throat, reveling in her sympathy. Tristan was moved by the depth of the bond between the two of them and, once again, he felt a mild twinge of envy. When at last she turned to face him, he was stricken to see tears in her thick lashes.

"He's been a fine friend to me," she said. "For so long, there was nobody to talk to but him. I don't think I could bear it if he—if he died."

Tristan would have touched her, if his hands hadn't been dirty. More than anything in the world, he wanted to reassure her, and give her whatever comfort he could. "He'll be all right," he said hoarsely, and lifted Spud carefully off the table and set him on the floor. The animal retreated to the kitchen hearth, where he lay down on the hooked rug with a whimper of self-pity and closed his eyes.

When Tristan came back in from scrubbing off the liniment and blood at the wash bench, he found that Emily had scoured the table, added wood to the stove and set a kettle of water on to heat. Now, she was merely measuring tea leaves into the chipped crockery pot that had come with the place, nothing more spectacular than that, but the sight of her in that shirt, with her braid dangling down her back, set him afire inside. Never, at any time in his life, had he wanted a woman as he wanted this one. He saw clearly that the secret feelings he'd cherished for Aislinn had been nothing more than shallow daydreams; this was something real and right. Something monumental.

And yet he barely knew her.

"I guess I'd best get back to the barn," he said. The words seemed to scratch his throat raw.

She looked at him in shy surprise and, unless

he was mistaken, hope. "Won't you stay a few minutes?" she asked. "I don't think I can go back to sleep right away." She poured steaming water into the teapot. "Sometimes a cup of tea helps, though it's said to be a stimulant—"

"Emily."

She stopped, looked at him again, waiting.

"This is improper, my seeing your—your limbs and all."

Incredibly, she laughed. "Day after tomorrow, we'll be married. And it's not as if we're, well, *doing* anything."

"It's the prospect of *doing something*," he retorted pointedly, "that I can't stop thinking about. Seeing you like that doesn't help, believe me."

Her mirth faded, though a spark of it lingered in her eyes. "Oh," she said, and the sound was small, hardly more than a breath.

He considered showing her the ring he'd bought earlier that day, at the general store, but if he did that, she might think he was trying to make her feel obliged. After all, he'd said, straight out, that he planned to seduce her. "I'd best go," he reiterated, and when he'd passed over the threshold, he stood looking up at the stars and silently cursing himself for every kind of idiot.

He returned to the barn, climbed up into the hayloft, and stretched out again. After a few minutes, he realized that he could still see the stars, the cracks in the roof were that wide. One good rain and the horses and all the hay would be drenched.

He went to sleep making a mental list of things he'd need to make the necessary repairs.

Emily took her time over her solitary cup of tea, convinced that she wouldn't get a wink of sleep even if she went back to bed immediately. Her mind, her senses, her very soul it seemed, were all full of Tristan—Tristan's mouth, Tristan's hands, Tristan's powerful shoulders and lean midsection.

Sitting at the kitchen table, where he had so skillfully attended to Spud's wounds only minutes before, she spread her fingers over her face and groaned. Then, peering through a space at the dog, she said in mock accusation, "How could you? I'm the one who feeds you and scratches you behind the ears and throws sticks for you to fetch. And what do you do when you get into trouble? You go to *him* for help!"

Spud gave another low whine, as if to make excuses for himself, but did not raise his muzzle from its position on his outstretched forelegs.

Emily finished the first cup of tea and poured herself a second one. There wasn't a grain of sugar in the house; Tristan didn't seem to use the stuff at all, but she hoped there would be a supply among the things the storekeeper had promised to deliver. Many of her best dishes required sweetening—rhubarb pie, for instance. She'd found a patch of the stuff growing in the deep grass out behind the barn, and wanted to put it to good use before the first hard frost.

Thinking about cooking calmed her nerves a little, and soon she put her cup in the sink, along with the teapot, put out all of the kitchen lamps but the one that would light her way upstairs, and retired to the room she would be sharing with Tristan after Sunday.

The idea stopped her in midstride. He had sworn he wouldn't force himself upon her, and she knew he would keep his word, as much for his own sake as for hers. But she hadn't asked if sleeping beside him was part of the bargain.

In the middle of the stairway, she laid her free hand to her bosom, fingers splayed, and tried to recover her composure by drawing and releasing slow, deep breaths. The thought of lying in Tristan's bed, with him right there next to her, maybe *touching* her, either by accident or by design, sent a terrifying surge of pleasure rushing through her. Suppose she saw him naked? He hadn't promised to behave modestly, after all....

Wide awake again, Emily went back downstairs to get her book. It was, she thought ruefully, going to be a very long night.

Emily was pleased, the next morning, to meet the storekeeper, Dorrie McQuillan. As she began unloading the wagon full of supplies, the woman explained cheerfully that she was Shay's older sister. Her manner was so open and friendly that Emily felt completely accepted, and that was a new and delightful sensation.

Emily introduced herself and set to helping with the carrying. She was feeling guilty, staying inside the house that day, dressed in calico, while Mr. Polymarr and the Indians looked after her sheep. Tristan was on the roof of the barn with Fletcher, making repairs with a hammer and nails and scraps of wood he'd found in one of the sheds.

"It's time he found himself a woman," Dorrie said, with a nod toward the barn, where Tristan's shirtless form was disturbingly visible. Emily hadn't worked up the courage to ask him if he expected to share the master bedroom and walk around in a state of undress.

"It's a business arrangement," Emily felt compelled to say. There must have been a dozen boxes in the back of that wagon; Dorrie climbed up, agile as any man in her practical riding skirt, and began shoving them into reach.

"Sure it is," Dorrie replied, without sarcasm. Still standing in the wagonbed, she looked Emily over critically. She was a plain soul, too tall and too slender by common standards of beauty, but she radiated some inner quality that made Emily want to know her better. "I reckon those ready-mades Aislinn sent along will fit you just fine," she said.

Emily was suddenly self-conscious, uncomfortably aware of her shabby dress, and though it chafed her pride sorely to accept charity, she could hardly wait to see what Dorrie had brought. "How is Aislinn? And the baby?"

"They're both just fine," Dorrie said, getting out of the wagon as nimbly as she'd gotten in. "Baby's delicately made, like her mama, but she's strong, too. There's so much life in her, you can feel the heat of it, little scrap of a thing that she is."

They took the last of the wooden boxes into the house.

"Will you stay for tea?" Emily asked. She would be frightfully let down if Dorrie refused, but she tried not to show it.

"I can't be gone long," Dorrie said, as she took a seat at the table, casting a curious glance at Spud, who was still languishing like an invalid on the hearth. "I'm running the store all by myself, with Aislinn in her confinement. Shay's right; it's time we hired on some help."

"Confinement" seemed a strange term, to Emily, for such a wonderful experience as bringing a child into the world. Busily, she rummaged through the groceries until she found a good-sized sack of sugar, and set the tea to brewing. Later, she would bake the rhubarb pies, to serve with supper, but for the moment there was nothing to offer Dorrie but tea.

"Where's home?" Dorrie asked. By then, Spud had crept over to rest his head on the bench beside her, and she was gently stroking his head, but her kindly gaze was fixed on Emily.

She didn't know exactly how to answer the question. She'd never in her life had a real home, until now. "Here," she said, at some length, and in such a quiet voice that Dorrie leaned forward a little to hear it. As far as she was concerned, the ranch was indeed hers, whether she became Tristan's wife or not.

Dorrie seemed satisfied with the reply. "Looks like this dog met up with a bee-stung grizzly," she observed. "Poor creature."

Emily recalled how Tristan had taken care of Spud, touching him gently and murmuring soothing words, even when the animal growled and bared his teeth. "Tristan says he'll be all right," she ventured.

"Of course he will," Dorrie confirmed.

After that, they drank tea and chatted a while, and Dorrie told the whole story of Shay and Aislinn's courtship, complete with dynamite and gunfire. It was, Emily thought, better than one of her books.

Perhaps an hour had gone by when Dorrie stood up and said she had to be on her way. She'd locked up the store before she left, and folks were bound to be breathing on the windows, which were impossible to keep clean, with all those fingers and noses pressed against them every day. And that was reckoning without the dust from the road which, according to Dorrie, never seemed to settle.

From the doorway, she pointed to a large brown-paper parcel, tied with twine. It was resting on the far end of the table, fat and intriguing. "That's from Aislinn," she said.

"Please thank her for me," Emily said.

Dorrie nodded and was gone.

Sorry to see her company depart, Emily set herself to unpacking the provisions and putting them in their proper places. There was flour, coffee, tinned vegetables, sacks of potatoes, turnips and onions, and a lot more besides, so the task took a long time. Emily saved Aislinn's package for last, and approached it cautiously when everything was done.

"It won't explode," Tristan remarked, from the doorway behind her, startling her by his presence. He'd put his shirt back on, at least. That was a mercy, because seeing him without it did unseemly things to Emily's insides.

She turned back to the package and took a step toward it. She was expecting a plain dress or two, well-worn and probably out of fashion, but her sense of anticipation was tremendous all the same. She wanted to draw out the experience as long as she could, even though it shamed her not a little to accept a gift of that sort. She wanted so much to provide for herself, but there was scant hope of that until the wool and mutton were sold.

After another glance at Tristan, she removed the string and folded back the heavy paper, slowly and very carefully. What she found inside made her draw in a sharp breath—dresses, *beautiful* dresses that showed hardly any wear at all. There was a white one, embroidered with tiny pink and green sprigs, and a black one, made of crisp, rustling sateen, softened by a collar and cuffs of delicate ivory lace. Another was bright yellow. There were lovely linens, obviously new, and stockings as well.

Emily was all but overwhelmed. Her knees went flimsy and she had to sit down on the bench next to the table to recover herself.

Tristan's hands came to rest on her shoulders, and though she knew he had meant to comfort her, the contact had an electrifying effect, rather like taking hold of a lightning rod during a storm. When she stiffened, he released his grasp, to her regret, but did not step away. She was very conscious of him, as hard and warm as the wall of a blast furnace. "I've got some business in town later today," he said. "Would you like to go along, and pay a call on Aislinn?"

The suggestion was a welcome one; she turned to look up into Tristan's face, smiling. "You don't think we'd be intruding?"

"Shay will be insulted if we don't make a fuss over that baby, and he'll be looking for us. Why don't you wear that yellow dress?" The blue heat in his eyes drew a flush to her cheeks, and she barely kept herself from covering them with her hands.

"I was going to bake some rhubarb pies," she said, and immediately felt stupid.

He grinned crookedly. "We won't be leaving for a few hours," he told her. "I've got things to do here."

She swallowed, and nodded, and was both relieved and bereft when he finally left the house to return to his work.

The rhubarb pies were cooling on the table when Tristan returned, in the middle of the afternoon, to say he was ready to head for Prominence. He'd evidently cleaned up in the bunkhouse, because his hair was damp and freshly combed, his boots were shined, and he was wearing a fresh cotton shirt and black trousers. The ever-present .45 rode low on his hip, an ominous reminder that there was a dark side to his nature.

Emily had changed while the pies were in the oven, and she was encouraged by the light she saw in Tristan's eyes as he looked at her. She grew flustered by his attention, however, and her hands trembled as she reached up to make sure her hair, wound up in a careful coronet at her nape, was firmly in place.

"Best put those pies away," Tristan said, with amusement in his voice. "If Spud doesn't get them, Polymarr or the kid will." He didn't wait for her to do it, but instead wadded up a pair of dish towels to protect his hands and stashed them, one at a time, inside the oven, which was now barely warm.

"Do you think they'll be safe here, with the sheep? Mr. Polymarr and Fletcher, I mean?" In some ways, Emily had been holding her breath, figuratively speaking, ever since the confrontation with the Powder Creek men. She almost wished they'd attack, and get it over with.

"Black Eagle and the others will look after things," he said. He had a lot of confidence, it seemed to her, in people he didn't know very well. Like her, for instance. Was he assuming that she was giving up her claim to the ranch by marrying him? Was that the true reason for his hasty proposal?

"Why should they?" She knew little enough about Indians, and she certainly sympathized with their plight, but she'd heard plenty of stories about their propensity for stealing.

His expression was grim, even hard. Here again was the dark Tristan, the inner twin to his normally sunny persona. "Because they've got families on the reservation, going hungry. They need what they earn."

Emily felt as though she'd been reprimanded, but that was of no consequence next to the starvation of a displaced and cheated people. "You care about them."

"Somebody ought to," he replied. "Are you ready, or not?"

Not for the first time in her life, Emily wished she'd kept her observations to herself. She followed him outside and hurried to keep up as he strode toward the buckboard, which was already hitched and waiting beside the barn. "I care, too," she protested, setting spaces between the words because he was moving so fast that she practically had to run to keep up.

"Do you?" He helped her into the wagon seat, went around behind, and climbed up beside her. "Then give them some of those damn sheep."

Emily was silent while he disengaged the brakes and brought the reins down lightly on the horses' backs. The buckboard lurched forward, and she hung on to the hard wooden seat with both hands. Finally, she found the words to form a reply. "I'll give them as many as they need," she said, "*if* you hand over the same number of cattle."

His blue eyes were narrow with suspicion as he looked down at her. "Do you mean that?"

She swallowed. She thought of the money she'd lose in wool and mutton sales, and mourned it, but the specter of starvation was far worse. She wouldn't be able to put a bite of food in her mouth, knowing that others were going hungry, practically at her elbow. "Yes," she said.

A grin broke over his face like a sudden sunrise. "Good," he said, "because I gave them twenty head this morning."

The true meaning of sacrifice impressed itself upon Emily. "You did not."

"I did," he insisted, fairly bursting with appreciation of his own generosity.

Emily sighed and bid a score of perfectly good sheep a silent farewell. "Will it be enough?" she asked, at great length. "To sustain them, I mean?"

Tristan was solemn again. "Probably not," he said. "They'll share with all their friends and relations. That can thin down the stew quite a bit."

After that, Emily was quiet, her mood dampened.

It was only when they reached the edge of town that her spirits rose a little. She hadn't been a part of a community since before the sheep came into her life, and it was lovely to see people striding along the wooden sidewalks, leaning in doorways, talking in front of the livery stable. She couldn't help noticing, though, that a few of them pointed fingers in their direction, and that Tristan's jaw was now set in a hard line.

They soon arrived at Shay and Aislinn's gate, and Emily thought the place was even more beautiful in the bright light of day, though it didn't have the same sturdy substance, she decided, as the ranch house did.

Shay called to them as Tristan was lifting Emily down from the wagon, and she saw him crossing the street from the marshal's office. His star-shaped silver badge gleamed on the lapel of his knee-length black coat, his hair was ruffled, and his grin was wide.

"Aislinn will be pleased," he said, coming to an easy stop before them. He nodded politely to Emily. "Ma'am," he acknowledged.

"Emily," she corrected.

He beamed. "Emily, then," he replied. Then he headed for the gate, unhooking the latch and standing back so his guests could pass. When they entered the front parlor, Emily was amazed to find Aislinn out of bed and neatly dressed in a black sateen skirt and starched white shirtwaist, the baby making a little bundle in her arms.

Her dark hair was swept up and held in place by tiny ivory combs, her brown-amber eyes sparkled, and her face glowed with happy color.

"Tristan—Emily—I'm so glad you came to call."

Tristan bent to kiss Aislinn's forehead. "All right," he said, with a soft gruffness that Emily might have begrudged, had the situation not been special, "let's have a look at this niece of mine."

Proudly, her eyes shining with motherly pride, Aislinn drew back the edge of the blanket to reveal a small, downy head, covered in fair hair. The child was delicate and lovely and yet, as Dorrie had said, there was a lively vitality about her, a distinct presence, even though she was but one day old.

Tristan lowered himself to one knee beside Aislinn's chair and grinned up at his brother. "Now *here*," he said, "is a breaker of hearts."

Aislinn laughed tenderly. "No," she said. "She will be kind, our Mattie. Kind and generous and sweet."

"And smart," Shay put in, taking Emily's arm lightly in one hand and ushering her to a nearby chair.

"Well, that goes without saying," Aislinn replied. Tristan got up, and she held the baby out to him. "Will you hold her?"

Tristan blushed and retreated a step, something Emily could not have imagined him doing before that moment. "I don't think I'm ready for that quite yet," he said.

"Coward," Aislinn challenged.

He would not be moved by insult, good-natured or otherwise, and perched on the edge of the settee, hat in hand, as if ready to bolt for the door. Within a few minutes, he and Shay went outside together, ostensibly to enjoy a celebratory cigar.

Aislinn smiled at Emily as warmly as if they'd been friends forever and said in a conspiratorial tone, "They're hiding out there."

Emily laughed. "Yes, I think you're right," she said. Her heart was warm and full. She looked down at her lovely yellow frock. "Thank you for sending me some of your things."

She assessed Emily thoughtfully. "That gown is very nice on you. When I wore it, I looked as though I had jaundice." Her face was soft with love for her husband and child. "What about you, Emily? Would you care to hold Mattie?"

"Oh, *yes,*" Emily said, and got to her feet.

Aislinn handed over the child with an easy trust that Emily would always cherish. She held the baby carefully, and sat down, and could not have explained why her eyes suddenly stung with tears. Silently, she offered a fervent prayer that the baby would always be loved and kept safe.

"Shay tells me you and Tristan are to be married on Sunday."

Emily looked up and met the other woman's gaze, blinking in vain. Her tears must have been obvious to Aislinn. "Yes," she said.

Aislinn's eyes sparkled with innocent pleasure. "Good. Tristan will make a fine husband. Reformed rogues usually do."

It came as no surprise to Emily that Tristan had been a rascal. He was handsome, and possessed of a potent sort of personal charm. Such men were popular with women, and generally took full advantage of the fact.

Her expression tender, she admired the baby, so small and solid in her arms, and yearned for one of her own. "He's a good man," she agreed. Then she remembered the broader situation and concern welled up inside her. She forced herself to look at Aislinn again. "How do you feel about sheep?" she blurted.

Aislinn stared at her, clearly baffled. "Sheep?"

"I have a flock. It's my understanding that the ranchers and a good number of the townspeople despise the poor creatures."

Aislinn rose, took the baby from Emily's arms and placed her carefully in the cradle that stood nearby. After covering her, she sighed and turned back to her guest. "These are honest, hardworking people," she said. "Give them time, and they'll come to their senses."

Emily squared her shoulders and raised her chin. "I've had experience with 'honest, hardworking people,' " she answered with some bitterness. "They acted as though I'd brought some dreadful plague into their midst."

Aislinn came to stand beside her, and rested one hand on her shoulder. "Was there no one to take your part?"

Emily shook her head, afraid to speak for fear she'd burst into wailing sobs, wake the baby, and make an utter fool of herself.

Aislinn's fingers tightened slightly. "Well, you have a family now. Things will be different."

Chapter

7

TRISTAN HAD BEEN GONE a lot longer than it should have taken to smoke a cigar, but Emily didn't mind. She and Aislinn exchanged life stories while the men were away, and a lasting bond was formed between them.

When Tristan did return to collect her, he had a thick packet of papers in the back pocket of his trousers and he was sporting an almost insufferable grin. He was pleased about something besides being an uncle, that was plain, but apparently he did not intend to confide his news any time soon. He said fond good-byes to his sister-in-law and niece—Shay was off making his rounds—and squired Emily outside to the wagon without a word.

Unsettled by the silence, benevolent though it was, she tried to make conversation when they were outside of town and moving toward the ranch at a good pace. "Shay and Aislinn are lucky to have that beautiful baby," she said.

"Yup," Tristan agreed, still grinning. He didn't even spare her a sidelong glance.

She cleared her throat and made another, more daring attempt. "I suppose you'll want children."

He made a clicking sound with his tongue to speed up the horses. "Yup," he repeated, and began to whistle softly through his teeth.

Emily gave up, but only temporarily. Whatever his secret was, she was bound to discover it in time. That it was probably none of her business anyway was wholly irrelevant.

Reaching the ranch, she was relieved to see that the sheep were grazing peacefully and that Fletcher and Mr. Polymarr were still in possession of their scalps. She began to hope that the danger from the Powder Creek men and others was past, though she knew that was overly optimistic. The animosity between cattlemen and sheep owners ran deep, and was by no means specific to Prominence and the surrounding area.

Holding the skirts of her prized yellow dress high, to avoid soiling the hem, Emily made her way to Black Eagle, who stood still as a statue in front of a cigar store, his sinewy arms folded. He smelled of smoke and leather and some sort of animal grease. There was no expression at all in his face as he looked down at Emily, but the marks of suffering and sorrow were etched deep into his flesh and bearing. He was gaunt, defeated, but still proud.

She smiled uncertainly, full of pity and well aware that that was the last thing he wanted or needed from anyone. How, she wondered, could she offer the man twenty head of sheep without sounding pompous? "You seem to be doing a fine job overseeing the flock," she said.

He didn't speak, and his features remained blank. She wished she'd consulted Tristan before approaching Black Eagle, at least asked how he'd given the tribe a score of cattle without injuring its collective dignity, but he'd been hardly more communicative than the Indian ever since they'd left town.

"Where is your village?" she persisted. Men were cussed creatures, it seemed to Emily, whatever their race, creed or color.

Black Eagle stared into her eyes for a long time, and she stared back. She'd approached him in good faith, the flock was hers, down to the last lamb, and she would not be intimidated. When he saw that she meant to stand her ground, he pointed to the west.

"There," he said.

Emily was mentally winded, just from the effort of pulling that one word out of him, but hers was a hearty soul, and she greeted it like a flash flood of scintillating conversation. "Do you have a wife? Children?"

"Three wives," Black Eagle responded, in perfectly clear English. There went the theory that he didn't speak the language. "Ten children."

Emily was taken aback. "That's—impressive." A great many mouths to feed, she reflected, and there might well be elders in Black Eagle's household as well, and indigent relatives. Most distressing of all, the group represented just one family, out of dozens or even scores. She was about to plunge in and offer him the pick of her sheep when Tristan interrupted.

There had been a profound change in his disposition since she'd seen him last. He was scowling, his eyes were narrowed and his jawline was clenched. Emily gaped at him, dumbfounded, with no earthly idea what she'd done to make him so angry.

It was Black Eagle who broke the uncomfortable silence. "Your woman talk plenty," he said.

Emily flushed with humiliation. She was about to protest that she was her *own* woman, and no one else's, that this was her land they were standing on, when a look from Tristan stayed her tongue.

"She raises sheep," he said, as though that explained her every shortcoming. His gaze had never left her face. "Go back to the house, Emily," he said crisply. "Right now."

Plainly, it would only make matters worse to argue, but she intended to blister Tristan's ears the instant they were alone. The very idea of his ordering her about that way, like a—like a husband! She would clear *that* little matter up, in no uncertain terms. Snatching a better hold on her skirts, she whirled and

121

flounced off toward the sanctity of the kitchen she had already begun to think of as her own.

Tristan watched his future wife's departure with undisguised appreciation. Lordy, but she was a little hellcat, all hiss and claw. Taming her might take years, and he looked forward to every moment of their life together, good, bad and middling. In time, he might even grow to love her, whatever that meant.

"Indian woman no talk," Black Eagle said firmly.

Tristan didn't see any reason to point out that Emily wasn't an Indian; that much was obvious. He heaved a great sigh of pretended resignation. "I guess I'll have to beat her," he said, though he'd never laid an angry hand on a woman before and never intended to do so.

Black Eagle nodded sagely. "It plain why white man take only one wife," he observed.

Tristan laughed. He knew Black Eagle had three mates, and the idea of Emily in triplicate was certainly enough to give a man pause, all right. "God help us all," he muttered, and steered the discussion in the direction he'd intended in the first place. "I bought a considerable spread of land today," he said. "I'll need all the men you can spare to help me run it. To seal the bargain, I'll give you twenty head of these sheep, your choice."

The Indian beckoned to one of the others and said something to him in dialect. The younger man nodded grimly, and the process of selecting the promised animals began. Tristan watched for a few moments, then turned on his heel and went back to the house, well aware that Emily would probably strip off a patch of his hide when he got there.

She was stirring something in a large kettle, her strokes powerful enough, in her dudgeon, to churn watered-down milk into butter. She glared at him and waited in obstinate silence for his apology.

He had no intention of offering one, but he was grateful as hell that she hadn't been there to hear his bluff remark about beating her. "When you give an Indian a gift," he explained, folding his arms, "he feels obligated to give you something in return. If he can't, he loses his honor, and honor is just about all these people have left."

Her fury dissipated, but she set the bowl down with a thump. Tristan saw cornmeal batter inside, and his mouth watered. "You might have mentioned that before," she said, still huffy.

"It didn't come up in conversation."

She narrowed her gaze, suspicious again. "What did they give you, for the cattle?"

"Firewood," he said. "Enough to keep us warm until the turn of the century, probably. The women and kids are gathering it now."

She bit her lower lip. "I'm sorry."

He allowed himself the semblance of a grin and pointed at her in mock surprise. "You?"

"I almost made a terrible blunder. I was about to say to Black Eagle that I'd heard the people in his village were starving, and that he should take his pick of the best ewes." She pressed the back of one hand to her forehead and heaved a frustrated sigh. When she looked at Tristan again, her eyes were bleak. "Isn't there something the government can do?"

Tristan spat out a contemptuous laugh. "The government? No Indian in his right mind would trust a politician or a soldier. Not after being lied to so many times."

The idea must have come to her out of the blue; he saw it take shape in her expressive face. "Will you take me there?"

"Where?" he asked, though he had an awful feeling that he already knew the answer. Not for the first time, he wondered what forces had shaped this remarkable woman into the person she was.

"To the Indian village, of course," she answered, confirming his suspicions.

He ground his back teeth, making an honest effort to show patience. "No," he said, and it came out sounding like a bark, though he hadn't meant for that to happen. The ragtag band occupying the small village a few miles to the west was largely peaceful, but there were always renegades, and they played by their own rules. Like as not, if some of them were to come along and carry her off, the others would not interfere.

Her eyes widened. "Why not?"

"Because it's no place for you, that's why."

"You'll have to give me a better reason than that if you expect to persuade me."

What was it about this woman that made him dig in his heels? "I'm not trying to persuade you. I'm *telling* you not to go near that camp."

"And I'm telling you that I'm not one of your men, obliged to take orders from you. Have you forgotten that I have a valid claim on this land? It seems to me that I should have something to say about how things are done!" She picked up the bowl again, grabbed the wooden spoon and stirred with a vengeance. He hoped the cornbread would still turn out, because he had a powerful hankering for a good-sized piece, slathered with butter.

He deliberated for a few moments, then gave a little ground, though he told himself it was mostly for the sake of supper. He'd deal with the domestic property dispute later. "You might carry some sickness to them," he said. "They're vulnerable to things like that—especially the children."

She put down the bowl again and dusted her hands on the printed flour sack she'd tied around her waist for an apron. Her brown eyes had gone round again, and he knew he'd swayed her, though he wasn't particularly proud of the fact. Anyway, it was true that the tribes had been decimated by smallpox, cholera and typhoid, all plagues they rightly dreaded. "But I'm fine," she said.

He spoke quietly, his mind full of the horrors he had seen in his travels. "That doesn't mean they couldn't catch something from you. Or me. Or any of the rest of us. It's better to leave them be, Emily."

She sighed. "It doesn't seem right," she said.

He wanted to put his arms around her, but he was afraid to do that because then he wouldn't be able to resist kissing her, and who knew where that might lead. He didn't doubt his ability to turn away, but the price of restraint was high. He'd suffer for his chivalry, and he was more than miserable as it was. He was not used to that particular sort of sacrifice.

Without making a reply to her remark, he took his leave, still hoping there would be cornbread for supper. A minor consolation, but a consolation all the same.

Mr. Polymarr and Fletcher came inside to eat, just as they had the night before. Emily was touched by their attempts to groom themselves for the occasion, and she made them welcome, filling their coffee mugs repeatedly and making sure they got a share of the cornbread she'd baked to compliment the meal. Tristan consumed more of the stuff than four men could have held.

When she served the rhubarb pie, all three men took generous portions and surrounded them with ease. It struck Emily that cooking meals on a ranch might be a career in itself.

Presently, murmuring their thanks, Mr. Polymarr and Fletcher left the house, and Tristan insisted on washing up the dishes, just as he had done the night before. She went in to sit by the front-room fire, still brooding over the Indian women and children, their hunger and hopelessness vivid in her mind's eye. She could well understand Tristan's bitterness on their behalf, and it raised him in her estimation that he cared at all. Many white men spoke of the natives with disdain, as though they were less than human, and treated their livestock with more charity.

So far did Emily's thoughts carry her that it made her start when Tristan spoke. "I have something to show you," he said, in a quiet, almost shy voice.

She looked up at him, standing over her, his hair full of firelight.

He dragged the other chair over and sat down facing Emily. Then he handed her the packet of papers he'd been so secretive about earlier in the day.

Confused, she unfolded them, and drew in a sharp breath. The documents represented the deeds for the Powder Creek ranch, which the late owner had evidently acquired in parcels. "This represents a great deal of money," she said, for she was frightened of debt and nothing more sensible had come to her.

"I *have* a great deal of money," he replied, without arrogance. He seemed to be merely stating a fact. "We'll move up to the big house as soon as I've gotten rid of the present crew of ranch hands," he added.

To her, the house they were *in* was big. Furthermore, it was hers, by rights. She wasn't sure she wanted to leave it, even though she had been there a very short time, and although she moved her lips, she found herself utterly unable to speak. The Powder Creek place was probably very grand; suppose he came to regret taking her to wife, instead of a woman with elegant manners, money of her own, and all the attending social connections?

He squinted. "What's going on in that extraordinary brain of yours?" he asked.

Emily raked her lower lip with her teeth, searching her heart for the courage to answer him. "I'm wondering if you'll change your mind about me one day."

He leaned forward and kissed the tip of her nose. The gesture was wholly innocent, and yet, like all his other caresses, it shook her somewhere far within. "I don't believe I will," he said, as though that closed the discussion. "Do I have to sleep in the barn again tonight?"

Her pulses began to pound, an inner drumbeat that warmed her blood. "We must come to an understanding about that," she said bravely. Her voice was a mere squeak.

Tristan arched one eyebrow. "What sort of understanding?"

"I was—well, I was wondering whether we're going to sleep in the same bed. After we're married, I mean."

He couldn't quite suppress the grin that lifted his mouth at one corner. "Don't all married people share a bed?" he asked, and though she knew he was teasing her, that did nothing to calm her racing heartbeat.

She looked away, looked back. "We didn't. My husband and I."

That announcement struck him with a visible impact. "Not ever?"

Emily shook her head. "He was old. He wanted a servant, not a wife."

"Then you're a virgin?"

"Yes," she said, straightening her spine. Her dignity, such as it was, was all she had to cling to at the moment.

"That," he said, cupping her face in both hands, "is good news. Not that I would have thought less of you, because I wouldn't have. But I do like knowing that I'll be the only man who has ever taken you to his bed."

She was afraid he would kiss her, afraid he wouldn't. If he did, she couldn't be certain *what* she might say or do. She felt his breath fan warm and sweet over her mouth, setting her lips to tingling. "I don't—I don't know how," she faltered.

He brushed her lips with his own. "I'll teach you," he promised.

A hot tremor went through her. "You'd better go now," she said, pulling away from him and bounding out of her chair as though there was a hot coal on the seat.

He caught hold of her hand. "You don't have to be afraid," he told her. Then he pulled her down onto his lap, and she did not have the will to resist him. His tone was low, rumbling, mesmerizing. "The first time can be uncomfortable, but I'll never hurt you. I swear it."

She couldn't say anything, and though she

tried to summon the will to pull away, it simply wasn't there to draw upon.

"I'll make it good," he went on. With the back of his knuckles, he lightly, ever-so-lightly, brushed the fabric covering the hard points of her breasts. "Let me show you, Emily."

Her head was swimming; the fire was a flickering blur on the hearth, and every nerve in her body was alive with a need so elemental, so primitive, that it frightened her. "Tristan," she whimpered.

He bent his head to her bosom and nibbled softly at one of the hidden nipples, and in that moment she became a part of the fire. Then he gave a raspy sigh and set her back on her feet, holding her by the waist for the several moments it took to regain her balance.

"I'm sorry," he said, and the legs of his chair scraped the floor as he stood. The deeds to the huge ranch bordering his lay scattered on the rug, and Emily bent to gather them up so swiftly that she nearly fell on her head.

He steadied her again, this time grasping her shoulders.

She handed him the papers, taking refuge among the last shreds of her pride. "Why apologize?" she asked, with a slight edge. "You did say you planned to seduce me."

He folded the documents, tapped them against the palm of one hand. "I wouldn't respect myself at all if I didn't try," he said. "Do you mind if I go upstairs for blankets and a set of long johns? It's cold in the barn."

She averted her eyes and gestured generously toward the stairs. "Help yourself," she said, and he laughed hoarsely as he left her.

Emily had expected her ardor to cool by morning, but when Tristan came in for breakfast, without Mr. Polymarr and Fletcher, her attraction to him was as strong as ever. She served him coffee and salt pork and leftover cornbread, and he watched her with a smile in his eyes while he ate.

"You'll be going to Powder Creek this morning?" The question had the tone of a statement. A sort of bleak resignation came over her. "Alone."

"Black Eagle and a few of his friends are going to ride along with me," he said. "And Powder Creek is the Double Crescent now. It's part of this place."

There it was again, that subject they were both avoiding. It just seemed that there was always something more important to discuss.

"You're determined to get yourself killed," she accused, in a burst of fear, unable to keep up the pretense of being calm any longer. Tears burned in her eyes, and she blinked desperately to force them back.

Tristan rose slowly from the bench at the table and came to her, laying gentle hands on her shoulders. "On the contrary," he said, "I've never wanted to live more than I do right now. But there are times when a man has to stand up for what's his, and this is one of them."

She knew he was right, but that didn't make it any easier to send him off to deal with people who weren't above shooting him. She slipped her arms around his waist and laid her head against his chest, and he held her, tentatively at first, then with a sort of possessive strength. He placed a light kiss on her temple.

"I'll be back in no time," he said. Then he hooked a finger under her chin and raised her face so he could look into her eyes. "Don't fret, Emily."

She sniffled and nodded her head, and they both knew it was a lie. She *would* worry, terribly.

He'd only been gone for a few minutes when she hurried upstairs, put on the trousers and shirt she'd been wearing when she arrived a few days before, and made for the barn. Walter was there, in her stall, growing lazier by the hour in her idleness.

Emily pulled a bridle over the mare's head and mounted, not troubling with a saddle. Tristan and Black Eagle were well ahead, accompanied by five other men, and she followed, staying well behind them. Should Tristan spot her, he'd make her go back if he had to hog-tie her and throw her over a saddle, and she didn't doubt for a moment that he was capable of just such drastic action.

The ride grew steeper as she progressed, her heart thundering at the base of her throat. She was scared of what might take place at the former Powder Creek, and even more frightened of not knowing, not seeing for herself what was happening.

Eventually, Tristan and his companions disappeared from view, swallowed by the dense woods that banded the hill in oak and fir, maple and birch. The leaves were bright yellow and russet, just beginning to turn. Emily kept her distance, guided by the trail of hoofprints pressed into the soft ground. Beyond the trees was a high meadow, and she was forced to rein Walter in and wait at the edge of the forest. If she went farther, she would be out in the open and certain to be noticed.

The house Tristan had bought was the largest Emily had ever seen, a magnificent structure of natural stone, with a score of windows and a veranda that wrapped around one side of it like a steamboat rail. A windmill turned slowly in the breeze, and she could see a massive barn as well, and a corral full of fretful horses. It was plain that, like Emily herself, they smelled trouble, even though there was no one in sight besides Tristan and Black Eagle and the braves riding a short distance behind them.

Emily was jerked off the mare's back, striking the ground hard, and before she could cry out, a callused hand clamped itself over her mouth. She struggled, and the assailant dug his thumb and forefinger into the hinges of her jaw, giving her head a painful shake.

"Settle yourself down, little lady," an oily voice hissed. "I don't want to hurt you, but I will if I have to." Emily was swamped with fear, but there was a quiet place inside her, a calm place where reason held fast. She obeyed the command and went completely limp, hoping her captor would think she had fainted and release her.

It didn't work. He stuffed a wadded bandanna into her mouth the moment he moved his hand away, and then tied another around her head to secure the first. He bound her wrists behind her, then hurled her up onto the back of a horse with such force that for a moment she thought she would swallow the bandanna and choke to death.

She still hadn't had a good look at the man who had ambushed her, but she didn't need to see him to know he was one of the riders who had terrorized her two days before, when she and Spud and Mr. Polymarr were looking after the flock.

He mounted behind her, and she felt his sloppy bulk, smelled sweat and whiskey and rotting teeth. He forced his hat down onto her head, and it was as effective as a blindfold. Emily's stomach roiled, and she fought the urge to vomit, knowing she might well strangle if she lost control.

After a while, revulsion gave way to sorrow. Tomorrow was Sunday, the day she was to have been married, and now everything was ruined. She might be dead by dawn, or wishing devoutly that she were. They would use her, these outlaws, as a weapon, or as bait for a trap. Once they'd drawn Tristan in, they would surely kill him.

Emily reminded herself that she must not

panic. If she was watchful, an opportunity for escape might present itself, but hysteria—her first and most ardent inclination—could only work against her. And against Tristan.

Give me courage, she prayed, and centered her thoughts on the sanctuary she had found within herself.

The hairs on the back of Tristan's neck stood upright, and the horses pranced nervously. Black Eagle and his braves arranged themselves in a circle, facing outward, keeping their mounts under careful control.

Tristan drew his .45 and got down off the gelding. On the second floor of the house, he saw a curtain move, caught the glint of a polished gun barrel. Suddenly, all hell broke loose behind him, the Indians shrieking war cries and generally creating a disturbance.

Tristan used the distraction to make a run for the front door, and even then the ground behind him was peppered with bullets fired from the roof. He was glad to see, when he had a chance to look, that Black Eagle and the others had taken cover behind water troughs and at the edge of the house itself, evidently unharmed. They had guns, and they gave back as good as they got.

Two men tumbled down from the roof, dead before they hit the ground.

Tristan pushed open the heavy front door, using it as a shield. "There's nowhere to go from here," he called. "Throw your guns out the window and we'll take you in alive."

The reply was another spray of gunfire, riddling the door.

"Hell," Tristan muttered, frowning at the damage. He'd probably have to send to San Francisco for a replacement, or even Mexico.

"Where's your bride, Saint-Laurent?" someone yelled from the upper floor. "You seen her lately?"

A chill trickled down Tristan's backbone like a drop of January creek water. He would have liked to believe the bastard was bluffing, but his gut told him this was no idle taunt. He held up a hand, palm out, signaling Black Eagle and the others to hold their fire.

"If you've got something to say," he shouted back, "say it straight out."

Silence.

A stir at the edge of the meadow caught Tristan's eye, and he let out a long breath when he recognized Emily's mare, riderless, reins dangling. Until then, he'd thought she was at home, with Polymarr and Fletcher and the rest of Black Eagle's crew to protect her. Now he knew she'd followed him, and they had her.

Bile scalded the back of his throat. Dear God, those sons of bitches had her.

He took a few moments to collect himself. Then he stepped into the spacious entryway and fired three shots through the ceiling. Overhead, somebody howled, and Tristan reloaded.

"Where is she?" he demanded.

"You loco or somethin', shootin' up your own house?" It was an aggrieved bellow. Word of the purchase had gotten around, apparently.

"I'll burn it to the foundation if I have to," Tristan replied, and he meant what he said. He'd roast the truth out of them if that was what it took to find out where Emily was.

"How do we know you won't start shootin' as soon as we show ourselves?"

"You don't," Tristan replied. "Where is she?"

Chapter

8

WHEN THERE WAS A HITCH in the negotiations, Tristan figured it was time to take decisive action. He found an old newspaper next to a nearby fireplace, rolled it up, lit it with a match, and set the drapes in the front parlor ablaze. They made a dark, acrid smoke, and as the house filled, the two men who'd been hiding out upstairs came stumbling down, choking and swearing.

Tristan got them both by the collar and

flung them out the door. They pitched halfway across the veranda before landing, and when they hit the floorboards, he was there to send them flying again. They struck the dirt in a pile and squirmed there, howling as loudly as if they'd been shot full of arrows.

Several of the Indians rushed past into the house, presumably to put out the fire, while Tristan and Black Eagle stood over the whining no-accounts. Tristan shoved his .45 into the base of one man's skull, while planting a knee in the middle of his partner's back.

"One more chance," he said, his voice hoarse from the smoke inside the house. "That's all, and then there's going to be a mess the likes of which this country has never seen."

"We don't know where she is!" squealed the one in the greatest danger of getting the back of his head blown off. "I swear to God, they never told us!"

Tristan got the other one by the hair and yanked. Coupled with the pressure of his knee in the middle of the man's spine—if indeed he *had* a spine—it got his point across. "There's a line shack somewhere up in the hills," he bawled. "It's north of the Indian camp!"

Tristan ground the bastard's face into the dirt. "She'd better be all right," he warned, in a voice that would have frightened him, coming from someone else. "My friend Black Eagle is going to keep an eye on the both of you until I get back. As God is my witness, if there's so much as a scratch on that woman,

I'll jerk your insides out, set them on fire, and stomp out the flames." He stood up, and Black Eagle signaled two of his braves, who promptly bound the outlaws hand and foot with strips of rawhide.

"I ride with you," Black Eagle said staunchly, and Tristan could see by his expression that there would be no changing the man's mind. There wasn't enough time to work out an agreement anyway.

Tristan swung up onto his gelding and reined it toward the high country. Black Eagle was mounted as well, and he spoke to his men in an earnest undertone before catching up with Tristan.

"What did you just say?" He was only mildly curious as to whether or not the captives would be alive when they got back.

The Indian's black eyes glittered. "I tell them, if the woman-killers try to get away, shoot them." Black Eagle probably knew every fold and hollow of the hills above, and Tristan was glad to have his company, though he wouldn't have admitted as much. With this particular companion at his side, he had a much better chance of getting Emily back safe, though he would have preferred Shay.

He'd seen a half-dozen cabins in varying states of collapse while exploring in the mountains; some had housed miners, some the families of settlers who'd died out or given up long ago. Some were line shacks, where cowboys riding a fence line could get in out of a storm. Emily could be in any one of them, or none.

"We need dog," Black Eagle said, and for a moment, Tristan, riding hell-bent for nowhere, couldn't grasp the meaning of the statement. Then he remembered Spud, and wheeled the gelding around in a wide circle, racing back toward his own ranch house.

It probably took thirty minutes to get there, and Tristan begrudged every second of that time, but if he was going to find Emily he had to have the animal's help. The gelding was still moving when he dismounted, bounding into the house, slamming the front door open, taking the stairs two and three at a time. In his bedroom he found what he sought: the tattered serape Emily had been wearing when she entered his life.

He didn't have to whistle for Spud; the dog, though injured, sensed calamity, and he was pacing nervously back and forth on the rug at the base of the stairs, making a sound somewhere between a snarl and a bark, when Tristan came down. He let the animal smell the serape, and the result was more than he would have dared hope for—Spud shot through the gaping door like a Chinese rocket, and Tristan went stumbling after him.

Both he and Black Eagle rode full out to keep up with the dog, and even then they probably would have lost him if he hadn't been forced to slow down on reaching the timber line. Of course, they couldn't travel as fast either, and time was passing, and Tristan was about as scared as he'd ever been in his life.

His greatest fear was for Emily, of course;

her captors were just stupid enough to hurt or even kill her. Every atrocity he'd ever seen, and he'd seen plenty, replayed itself in his mind as he rode, with Emily as the victim. He felt stark, cold terror, and the messages rising from his gut were no comfort at all.

At last the dog paused, prowling along the edge of a ridge. His ruff stood out in bristles, and he snarled and yipped like a wolf with prey in its sights, waiting impatiently for the pack to catch up.

Tristan might have ridden straight down into the gully if Black Eagle hadn't extended an arm and stopped him by taking hold of the gelding's bridle.

They dismounted, and Black Eagle led the horses farther back into the woods, after giving Tristan a warning glance. The shack below, a weathered board structure leaning far enough to one side that a stiff wind would blow it over, was clearly occupied. There were two horses out front, and a ribbon of smoke curled from the crooked chimney pipe, making a gray smudge against the sky.

Black Eagle returned, crouched beside Tristan. "No guards," the Indian said. By then, Tristan had to restrain the dog to keep him from flinging himself at the cabin, a pretty good indication that Emily was inside and probably alive, too, though there was no telling what shape she was in. He closed his eyes for a moment, and silently implored a God he had long since stopped believing in to protect her.

"Not worry," Black Eagle said, in a whisper. "She talk them to death."

He'd no more than uttered those words when the shack's rickety door creaked open and one of the Powder Creek men came outside, unbuttoned his pants, and took a long piss in the brush at the side of the cabin.

Tristan squinted, straining for a glimpse of Emily through the open door, and in that moment he relaxed his hold on Spud just long enough for the dog to break free and dash, growling ominously, for his target. The cowboy, still holding his pecker in both hands, was taken by surprise and gave a little whoop of alarm that might have been funny, under other circumstances.

The dog was on him, at his throat, when the second man came out of the shack. He had Emily crushed against him, facing forward, and his pistol probed deep into the side of her neck. She looked pale and understandably rumpled, but otherwise unhurt, and Tristan's relief was so great that he almost forgot she was in imminent danger of being shot to death.

"Come on out, Saint-Laurent," the big man called, getting his name right, and Tristan recognized him then. Once a Texas Ranger, Elliott Ringstead had gone bad a long time ago, and made himself a reputation as a thief and murderer of no little imagination and enterprise. He was the one man Tristan had ever tracked in vain, and the bounty on his head had probably compounded half a dozen times over the years. "No sense hidin'. I know you're out there."

The man with his pants down was still wrestling with the dog, and shrieking like a frightened spinster all the while. Emily looked down and spoke to the animal in a quiet, firm tone. Reluctantly, Spud withdrew, but he didn't go far, and he kept looking from one outlaw to the other, awaiting his chance.

Ringstead cocked the pistol and thrust it harder against Emily's neck. "You gonna make me shoot her, Saint-Laurent? A ladies' man like you? Why, I don't believe it!"

"All right," Tristan shouted back. He stood and tossed the .45 down the hillside, and it struck the ground with an audible thump. "Let her go." He started the descent, his hands raised.

Emily's bright eyes widened with alarm when she saw him, then she squeezed them shut and shook her head slightly. Her lips formed a soundless word, once, then again. "No—no."

"You know, Saint-Laurent," Ringstead drawled, "I've always wished I had your way with the women. This one here's uncommon pretty—you outdone yourself this time, yes indeedy."

"I should have tracked you down a long time ago," Tristan said evenly. He met Emily's gaze and saw a reprimand there; she had not wanted him to come out of hiding. Of course, he couldn't have done otherwise, and right then her opinion on the matter was of little concern anyhow. "I believe the posters read, 'Dead or

Alive.' The first will do as well as the second."

Ringstead laughed, showing a row of tiny brown teeth and a lot of gum. "Looks like you're goin' to be the one that's dead," he observed. With the toe of his boot, he gave his partner a nudge calculated to bruise. "Get up, Homer. In case you ain't noticed, we got the upper hand here."

Emily flashed a warning look at Tristan and then bit said hand with as much force as she could. Ringstead bellowed a curse, and she brought her heel down hard on his instep for good measure. Tristan made a desperate dive for Emily and flung her to one side, and during that interval Ringstead recovered enough to raise and sight in the pistol. He was so close there was no need to take aim; he simply drew back the hammer.

"No!" Emily screamed.

A shot was fired, and Tristan waited for it to hit him. And waited.

Ringstead went down instead, graceful as a dancer, despite his bulky, awkward build, a crimson stain spreading across his chest and belly. Tristan realized that Black Eagle had just saved his life, but a shout from Emily brought his attention to the fact that the partner, heretofore wriggling on the ground, twisted up in his own pants, had gotten hold of the discarded .45.

"Put it down," Tristan said calmly.

Emily had collected Ringstead's gun, and she was standing over the other man, the pistol steady in her hands. "If you pull that trigger," she told Homer, with bitter sincerity, "I will kill you."

The outlaw considered his situation and then handed the .45 over to Tristan, butt first. Tristan jerked the man to his feet and tossed him to Black Eagle, who was ready with more rawhide to secure the prisoner's hands and feet, but his attention, all of it, was fixed on Emily.

"Are you hurt?" he asked. They might have been alone, for all the notice he took of the world around him; it was merely a pounding, blurry void, an aura of light at the edges of his vision.

She flung herself against him, hurled her arms around his neck and held on like a drowning swimmer. "They were saving me for after they killed you," she replied, trembling against him. "Oh, Tristan, thank God you're safe!"

He held her very tightly and closed his eyes for a moment, dizzy with relief. Then he thrust her to arm's length and looked her over again. His fear had crested and then ebbed, but his mind was still spinning in the backwash. He opened his mouth to tell her precisely what he thought of her reckless interference, but she was alive, and unhurt except for a few bruises and scrapes, and that made the rest of it unimportant. He wrenched her close again and buried his face in her hair.

Black Eagle leaned over Ringstead's body, peering at him curiously. "You knew this man?"

Tristan let Emily go at last and turned to look

down at the dead outlaw. "I spent two years hunting him," he answered numbly.

Emily came to stand beside Tristan, gazing anxiously into his face. She was a tough little thing; many other women would have swooned, or at least burst into tears, during and after such an ordeal, but she hadn't given Ringstead's corpse a second look. "Hunting?" she echoed.

He had not wanted her or anyone else—not even Shay—to know about his years as a bounty hunter, little better than a hired gun. But the choice had been taken from him; he would have to tell the tale, admit that for most of his life he had made his living by tracking men like any other prey, dragging them to the authorities when they would surrender, killing them when they wouldn't. He had in fact enjoyed the hunt, the way he would a challenging chess match or a high-stakes game of cards, and as long as they'd been the first to draw, he hadn't minded killing them, either.

"Tristan?" Emily prompted, when he didn't speak. Didn't look at her.

Finally, she turned away to crouch down in front of Spud, ruffling his fur gently and praising him. He gave a series of happy yips and licked her face until she laughed and struggled back to her feet.

Only later, when Ringstead's body was strapped facedown onto his horse, and his more fortunate partner perched in his own saddle, with his hands bound to the saddle horn, did she press the point. Since she was riding behind Tristan, her arms tight around his waist, her mouth close to his ear, he could not pretend he didn't hear her question.

"Are you going to tell me who you are?"

"Yes," he answered, after a long time. "Later. At home."

Mercifully, she settled for that.

The ranch house was a blessed sight to Emily, for she had not expected to see it again. Near the kitchen door, Tristan handed her down from the horse's back without dismounting himself. Black Eagle kept a tactful distance, the exhausted Spud sprawled across his lap like a sack of grain.

"Shall I hold supper?" she asked.

He sighed and shook his head. "No." He indicated the dead man and the prisoner with a grim nod. "Shay will have a lot of questions, Emily. Black Eagle and I left a few bodies scattered around today, and that calls for some explaining."

She pressed her lips together briefly, biting back a protest, and then managed a wobbly smile. "Thank you for coming after me, Tristan. Even though it was a stupid thing to do."

He gave her a wry look. "We'll discuss stupid things to do when I get back," he said. "Save me a slice of that rhubarb pie, unless Fletcher and Polymarr have already gotten to it."

Her eyes burned, and she blinked a couple of times. Spud leaped down from Black Eagle's horse and limped over to her, dirty and sore and all but spent by the afternoon's heroics. "Hurry back," she said to Tristan, and started toward the house, walking slowly so the dog could keep up.

There was plenty to occupy her hands, but her mind was with Tristan while she washed Spud's wounds again, and treated them with medicine, while she took a sponge bath in the spare room and changed into another of the dresses Aislinn had given her. Downstairs, in the kitchen, she peeled potatoes and turnips and put them in a pan of cold, salted water to be boiled later.

The sun was setting when Fletcher rapped shyly at the open door and found her sitting at the table, her hands folded in front of her, staring into space. She started, then summoned up a smile.

"I brung you these here grouse," he said, and held up a brace of birds, already plucked and cleaned. "They're good when you fry 'em in bacon grease."

Emily had not thought beyond the turnips and potatoes, and she was genuinely pleased by the boy's gift and the generous spirit behind it. "How wonderful," she said. "Thank you. If you'll give me half an hour, I'll have a meal on the table."

Fletcher swallowed, and she knew he was going to ask about Ringstead and his companion. There was no way to stem the question; it was a marvel that he'd waited this long to approach her. "Looked like there was trouble up in the hills today. Sounded like it, too."

Emily met his eyes. "Everything's fine now," she said soothingly, and hoped she was telling the truth. She had a feeling that her whole future depended upon what Tristan would say when he came home that night. "I'd better get busy," she said, with forced good cheer, "if we're going to have supper anytime soon."

Fletcher hesitated, then went out. Spud, back in his spot in front of the kitchen hearth, whimpered a comment, then closed his eyes for a well-earned rest.

Soon, the grouse were cooked and the potatoes and turnips were drained and steaming in the middle of the table, still in the cast-iron kettle. She went out to the pasture, where the sheep were bedded down for the night, watched over by their Indian shepherds as well as Fletcher and Mr. Polymarr.

Looking over her flock, Emily knew her problems were far from over. Maybe what Tristan was going to tell her about himself would change things, and maybe it wouldn't, but either way she was still an outsider, land or no land, house or no house. A sheep owner smack in the middle of cattle country, a pariah of sorts. Would there never be a place for her?

"Time to eat," she said quietly.

"Them Injuns claim they're entitled to their pick of the sheep," Mr. Polymarr fussed. He would not have been happy without a crisis, but Emily was ready for peace. "Twenty of 'em, no less!" He squinted at her as they walked toward the square of golden lamplight that was the kitchen door. "That true?"

"It's true," she said and, to his plain disappointment, did not elaborate.

When supper was over and Mr. Polymarr and Fletcher had taken their leave, the former having made repeated and hopeful reference to his fondness for rhubarb pie, making it clear that he would welcome a second helping, all to no avail, Tristan had still not returned from town, and his interview with Shay.

Emily heated water, washed the dishes, and watched the clock. It was after nine when Tristan finally came in, looking weary and strained. He tossed his hat onto a side table and thrust a hand through his hair.

"I've kept your supper warm," she said. They might, she reflected, have been married for twenty years, such was the sense of ease and quiet acceptance between them. To her way of thinking, any trouble that fell to him would fall to her in an equal portion.

He nodded. "Thanks." He went outside to wash while she built up the fire in the cookstove to brew fresh coffee. When he came in, she took his plate from the warming oven, with its gleaming chrome front, and set it on the table.

The food looked a little shriveled, but Tristan didn't seem to mind. He ate with good appetite, saying hardly anything, and some of the familiar twinkle came into his eyes when he saw the generous serving of pie she'd saved for him.

She poured his coffee and waited and, in time, her patience was rewarded. He pushed away his empty pie plate and looked at her steadily. She knew he was almost ready to tell her about his past, and braced herself to hear it.

"That was a good meal," he said. "Thank you, Emily."

She sat down across from him and folded her hands. "You're welcome," she said, and then lapsed into an expectant silence.

He heaved a heavy sigh. "Shay wouldn't let me out of his office until he'd gone through every wanted poster he had, in case I turned out to be a fugitive. I'm afraid things are a little awkward between my brother and I, just now."

"Are you?" Emily asked. "Wanted, I mean?"

A shadow moved in his eyes. "No," he said. "I always managed to stay on the right side of the law. I was a bounty hunter, and before you say that's a respectable trade, let me tell you that you're wrong. I was a gunslinger. I took a lot of men in alive, but I killed just as many. I thought I'd left that life behind, until today." He sighed. "I should have known better. I've got enemies out there—fathers, brothers, friends of the people I shot down or sent to prison. What happened today could happen again. And again."

She held her breath, then blurted, "I won't go, if that's what you're about to suggest."

"Emily, it isn't safe here. Never mind the

cattlemen. *I'm* more of a threat to you than they are. I'll pay you for the land, for the sheep—"

She folded her arms. "Are you going back on your word?" she interrupted.

He stalled by reaching for his coffee and taking several sips. Finally, he had no choice but to answer. "Were you listening to me?" he countered, leaning forward. "I've *killed* people, Emily. Dozens of them. And it isn't over, because there's always going to be somebody like Ringstead, looking for revenge. Or just wanting to prove something."

She considered that statement. "I'll take my chances," she said. "It's not as if I expect an easy life, after all. Just a good one."

He looked bewildered for a moment; then he laughed ruefully and shook his head. A mischievous smile touched his lips. "Does this mean I don't have to sleep in the barn?"

"I couldn't very well ask you to spend the night out there after the day you've had," she said, and watched as his eyes widened. "You can have your own bed back, and I'll sleep in the spare room."

His face fell slightly, but he was quick to recover. "You're very generous," he allowed. He raised both arms and stretched, and there was something so earthy and sensual, so masculine, in that simple motion that Emily was deliciously discomfited.

"Well!" she said brightly, getting to her feet and words spilling out of her and scattering as if someone had turned her upside down, like a milk can full of marbles, and given her a shake. "It's been quite a day, hasn't it? I believe I'll turn in. Good night, Tristan."

He reached across the table and caught her hand in his. Then, leaning forward slightly, he brushed a light kiss across her knuckles. "Good night," he said, in a low tone that lodged inside her, sweet and warm and spiky. The sensation was one of pleasure, rather than pain, but it left her even more shaken than before.

He held her hand a moment longer, clearly as aware of the charge passing between them as she was, then reluctantly let her go. "You take the main bedroom," he said, and his voice raked the smoldering embers inside her to full flame. "You have my word that I won't bother you."

Emily turned and fled, mostly to keep from blurting out that she wanted him to lie beside her, husband or not. It did not even matter to her that he was a self-professed gunslinger with a string of killings behind him.

She did not sleep well that night, and thus, when the delegation of ranchers arrived just after dawn, she was dressed and ready to face them. Quick as she was, Tristan, clad in hastily donned trousers and his undershirt, was there before her. His suspenders dangled at his sides and his hair was mussed, but he was wearing boots and the gunbelt that seemed such an integral part of him.

There were a dozen mounted men in the dooryard, all of them grim and armed with rifles.

153

Their faces were shadowed by the brims of their hats, but they'd made no attempt to disguise themselves. Emily glimpsed varied brands as the horses fidgeted, sensing conflict the way animals do.

"We can't have them sheep in amongst our cattle," the lead man announced. He was probably in his fifties, with a gray stubble of beard and a lean frame that bespoke years of hard work. "You ought to know that as well as anybody, Saint-Laurent."

It angered Emily that the man would address Tristan, when the sheep were hers alone, but there were more important things at stake, so she held her tongue.

Tristan pulled up one suspender, then the other, giving each one a little snap for emphasis. Standing beside him, Emily saw that his gaze had locked implacably with that of the spokesman, and understood some of what the men he hunted down must have felt, facing that quiet, unbending certainty. "As long as these sheep stay on my property, I don't see where they're any concern of yours."

Emily felt a surge of pride and, at one and the same time, she was as frightened as she'd ever been in her life. Even with Black Eagle and his men, and Mr. Polymarr and Fletcher, Tristan was outgunned. It wouldn't matter much who won or lost, she reasoned, if he died in the skirmish. Nothing mattered as much as saving his life. She stepped in front of him, as if to form a shield.

"I'll move on," she said quickly, looking up

into the rancher's shadowed face, trying to find a human being there. "I'll surrender my claim. I'll take my sheep and leave, right away. There's no need for any shooting."

Tristan set her aside, and she sensed both anger and respect in the way he gripped her shoulders. "She's not going anywhere," he said, "because we're about to be married. But Emily's right about one thing: there's no call to start a range war. You men get down off your horses and come inside. We'll have breakfast and talk this thing through."

Emily held her breath.

The ranchers argued among themselves for a time, but finally they dismounted. Although they sheathed their rifles in the scabbards affixed to their saddles, they were all wearing side arms. Tristan led the way into the house, and Emily trembled inwardly as she walked beside him.

The men took their places at the long table, filling up the benches on both sides. Tristan brought a chair from the other end of the house and sat at the head, as dignified, even in his undershirt and suspenders, as a judge calling a courtroom to order.

Emily busied herself brewing coffee and starting a batch of flapjacks, but she was alert to every nuance of word or movement at the table. She took note, with a degree of consolation, that once they'd shed their hats and long, dusty coats, the ranchers were but ordinary men, one or two well into their later years and graying, their faces weathered and rugged, a few just sprouting their first whiskers. Most, though, were someplace in between.

They were family men, almost without exception, fathers and husbands, brothers and sons. Seated at her table, with mugs of coffee steaming before them, they did not seem so fearsome as they had out front, mounted and carrying rifles at the ready.

"You ain't got enough land to run sheep and still keep 'em off the open range," a bearded man challenged.

Tristan sat easily in his place of command, his hands cupped loosely around his coffee mug, his tone and manner affable. "I own this place—" He paused and glanced at Emily. "—or at least, my future wife does. The Powder Creek spread is mine now. To my way of thinking, that's plenty of space to accommodate a band of sheep."

"Since when are you so fond of them woolly critters?" a younger man asked. "I thought you was a cattleman, like the rest of us."

"I am," Tristan said. His eyes met Emily's as she came to the table and began to set enamel plates in front of the men. She was shaking a little, marveling. He'd conceded that the original ranch was hers. "The sheep belong to my bride here. Because they're hers, I'm willing to see them through the winter and protect them like I would my own stock."

A brief, pensive silence fell, then the ranchers began to stir and murmur again, and reminded

Emily of a covey of old ladies gossiping over a quilting frame. Except, of course, for the guns on their hips.

"I reckon we can wait till spring," one man said, at last. "See how things go."

Emily's knees went weak with relief, and while she was cooking and serving up the pancakes, her heart sang.

Chapter

9

THE CHURCH WAS PRACTICALLY empty that afternoon, when Emily and Tristan stood up before the preacher to exchange their wedding vows. Shay served as best man, while Aislinn lent her support from the front pew. Although she had insisted that she was well enough to stand beside Emily, her husband had insisted otherwise. For the sake of the peace, she had complied.

Emily was moved when Tristan produced a golden wedding band at the proper point in the ceremony and slipped it onto her finger. She promised herself that she would buy a matching ring for him, come the summer, when the lambing and shearing were done and there would be money to spend.

When the preacher pronounced the words that bind man and woman together in the sight of God and humanity, Emily nearly swooned with joy, excitement, and relief. Tristan took a steadying grip on her arm and they turned together to accept congratulations from Aislinn and Shay.

"I'll be a good wife to him," Emily said, when Shay planted a brotherly kiss on her forehead. Although he smiled, the expression in his eyes was serious, and she knew the strain between him and Tristan had not abated.

"I know," Shay answered gruffly.

Tristan had taken a seat beside Aislinn on the pew, and she was embracing him in gleeful celebration. Emily felt a tug in the region of her heart, looking at them, and hoped she would be in her sister-in-law's place one day soon, with a genuine marriage and a child.

A commotion outside distracted them all; Shay and Tristan exchanged a closed look that troubled Emily and headed down the aisle together. Both wore the ever-present gunbelt and pistol, and neither Emily nor Aislinn failed to notice that they'd thrust back their coats on one side, in order to draw unimpeded. They hurried after their husbands.

Outside, the sunshine was bright, the air crisply cool. More than twenty mounted men had gathered in front of the church, pistols in hand. Emily recognized some of them: ranch hands, formerly employed at Powder Creek. It was plain from their bloodshot eyes, flushed faces and unkempt clothing that they'd been consuming ardent spirits, and that the indulgence had not improved their general attitude.

A man spurred his horse through the center of the gathering and drew up within a foot of where Shay and Tristan stood, shoulder to shoulder, each with a hand resting on the well-worn butt of his .45.

"You think you can turn us out like so many Injuns and run sheep on Powder Creek land?"

"That's exactly what I think," Tristan answered. "The place is mine now, and I'll do as I like with it."

The man blinked, obviously confused as to who was whom. Then he glared blearily at Tristan. "We'll kill you if we have to," he said, and Emily's throat closed so tightly that she couldn't breathe. Aislinn gripped her fingers and squeezed hard, crunching the bones together.

"You're never going to get a better chance than right now," Tristan replied. They might have been discussing the price of oats for all the emotion he showed, and his hand was all too steady on the handle of his pistol.

"You can't get us all," another man put in.

"That may be so," Shay interjected, "but we can take a fair number of you with us."

Emily started forward at that, a protest on the tip of her tongue, but Aislinn jerked her back with surprising strength, for someone who had so recently given birth.

If she could have spoken, Emily would have cried out that the men could have her sheep, could do anything they wanted, if only they would leave Tristan and Shay alone. She did not wish to become a widow on the very day of her wedding, or ever, for that matter.

"Stay out of this," Aislinn whispered fiercely.

Emily's pulses pounded, and it took all the self-control she possessed not to wade straight into the center of the fray, but she was not without a measure of common sense. The situation was a powder keg, and one impulsive move could bring on an explosion.

A flash from an upstairs window of the hotel caught her eye, and Emily squinted in disbelief. An old woman was bending over the sill, sighting in a rifle with obvious expertise. Cowhands came out of the Yellow Garter Saloon, while other men appeared in front of the feed-and-grain and the livery stable.

Emily recognized several of the ranchers who had dined at her kitchen table that very morning. The group converged to form a broad half-circle around the angry riders.

One of them stepped forward and spoke in a strong voice. "Don't you boys go thinkin' you can shoot the marshal and ride out without takin' the consequences," he said. It was Elmer Stanton, the gray-haired fellow who'd eaten three stacks of pancakes. He served as the spokesman, just as he had earlier in the day.

"You ride out of here and let us handle our own troubles."

"But they've got sheep!" one of the mounted men argued.

"Like I said, that's between them and us. It's got nothin' to do with you, now that you ain't part of the Powder Creek outfit anymore. And now, well, it's time you boys moved on to someplace where you ain't got a reputation. We've got no use for you around here."

Emily leaned against the doorframe, her fingers and Aislinn's interlaced as they waited. The golden wedding band, so recently donned, seemed to sear her flesh. She wanted nothing in that moment—*nothing*—but to go home with Tristan, her husband. To be alone with him, to lie in his arms, to lay her head upon his chest and hear the strong, steady beat of his heart. Knowing that any one of the men gathered in the street had the power to still that heart forever only made the prospect more poignant.

Tears burned in her eyes, and she blinked them back furiously.

"I ain't gettin' myself kilt over a few sheep," one of the younger riders announced, in a clear voice. "There's work up in Montana. I'm headed that way, if anybody wants to come along." With that, he wheeled his gray speckled pony away from the others, and the barrier of armed men who'd come to intercede parted to let him pass.

It was the lead man who shot him, square in the back. Emily saw a puff of smoke from the old woman's rifle before she heard the report of a second bullet, and watched in horror as the slayer fell forward, out of the saddle, dead before he struck the ground.

For a few moments, panic reigned; pistols and shotguns were brandished, and Emily was terrified that there would be more shooting.

Then Shay's yell rose over it all. "Damn it, don't anybody fire another shot! This thing has gotten out of hand as it is!"

Several of the first man's friends had gone to check on him; he was wounded, and there was copious blood, but when they hoisted him to his feet and shuffled him off in the direction of the doctor's office, it seemed likely that he'd survive. The second one, the ringleader, was not so fortunate. Tristan crouched before him and pressed two fingers to the base of the man's throat.

"He's dead," he said, addressing Shay.

"Damn it all to hell," Shay replied, irritated. Then he stepped toward the remaining riders. "Any of you fellows want to pass the night in my new jail? If you don't, then I'd advise you to get out of here before I lose my temper!"

Emily dared to glance at Aislinn.

"Isn't he wonderful?" whispered the latter.

Emily smiled, but she wasn't thinking about Shay, either; her mind was on Tristan. He was alive and unhurt. He was her husband. "Oh, yes," she agreed, and she wasn't talking about Shay. "There's no one like him, anywhere."

The riders scattered, however reluctantly, and Shay and Tristan went forward to confer with the ranchers who had come to their rescue. Emily, suddenly reminded of the strain her sister-in-law had been under, took Aislinn's arm. "We'd better get you home now," she said.

Aislinn nodded, and let Emily assist her to the house at the other end of the street, where the boys, Thomas and Mark, waited wide-eyed on the front step, while Dorrie looked after the baby inside.

"We heard shots," Thomas said, hurrying toward his sister. "Is Shay—?"

Aislinn ruffled her brother's thick chestnut hair. "He's fine. So is Tristan. There was some trouble, but things are fine now."

"Can we go see?" Mark wanted to know.

"Absolutely not," Aislinn answered. She was looking a bit wan, though Emily knew how strong she was, and figured she'd be right as rain after a few days of taking things easy. "You'll just have to wait until Shay comes home. He'll tell you the whole story, I'm sure."

The screen door squeaked on its hinges as Dorrie appeared on the threshold. "I see by your face that my brother is still among the living," she said to Aislinn, as coolly as if she'd been through the same ordeal a hundred times before. "The babe's sleeping like a little angel, but you look a mite the worse for wear." She came outside and, between the two of them, she and Emily got Aislinn inside and up the stairs to bed.

In the large kitchen, Dorrie brewed a pot of tea and joined Emily at the round oak table.

She glanced tellingly at the band on Emily's finger. "So he's taken a wife at last, has he?" she murmured, and for a few moments it was impossible to tell whether the older woman was pleased or displeased by this turn of events.

Emily twisted the ring round and round. Why didn't Tristan come and fetch her? Surely it was time to go home and—what *would* they do when they reached the ranch? She wished she were an experienced woman, knowledgeable in the ways of the flesh, but she was woefully ignorant in such matters.

A blinding smile broke across Dorrie's otherwise plain face. "It's time and past that Tristan Saint-Laurent settled down. He wants a family in the worst way, that young man. That's why he stayed on after he got his money back. His brother was here. He didn't want to leave Shay."

Emily bit her lower lip. She certainly understood Tristan's desire to be close to his only blood kin; it was not pleasant to be alone in the world, however self-sufficient one might be. "It would be a fine thing to have a brother or a sister," she said, and cleared her throat because her voice had turned rusty all of the sudden.

Briefly, Dorrie looked sad. "Usually," she agreed, and then her smile was back. "No sense in looking back," she said musingly, as though speaking to herself. She patted Emily's hand. "You have choices in life, for all that you're a woman. Choose to be happy, and you will be."

Aislinn had told Emily about Dorrie's lost love during their long conversation the day before, but she didn't want to ask about the choices the other woman had made.

Dorrie beamed. "You're wondering about me, aren't you? Whether or not I'm happy?"

Emily lowered her gaze briefly, embarrassed, and did not reply.

Her companion laughed. "Don't you fret, Mrs. Saint-Laurent. I've got a good life here in Prominence—Aislinn and Shay need me. There's the baby, and those motherless boys, to look after. The store takes up a lot of my time, too. I reckon I've got more to be thankful for than most."

It was the first time anyone had addressed her by her married name; she loved being called "Mrs. Saint-Laurent." Her mind was eased, too, at least where Dorrie's welfare was concerned. Hearing Tristan and Shay entering at the front of the house, her thoughts turned to other matters. She swallowed and looked away.

Dorrie patted her hand again. "You picked a good man," she said, in a reassuring whisper. "He'll know when to be gentle and when to be rough."

"Emily?" Tristan's voice rang through the house.

After a farewell word to Dorrie, she went to find him. They met in the dining room, stopped about ten paces apart, like gunfighters meeting in the street.

"Ready to go home, Mrs. Saint-Laurent?"

he asked. His voice was husky, and his blue eyes burned into her, making promises. It was only midafternoon, but autumn was coming on fast, and it would be dark in a few hours.

She nodded, suddenly shy. Tristan had sworn he would not force her into conjugal relations, and she trusted him wholeheartedly. Still, he had made it clear that he expected to lie beside her in their marriage bed, and he'd never been secretive with regard to his intention to seduce her. She wanted him, perhaps even loved him, but the reality was a fearsome thing. Suppose she was a disappointment to him? Suppose intercourse was painful and degrading, as some women hinted that it was?

Seeming to read her thoughts, he took her hand and smiled. "No hurry," he said softly, and led her outside. The wagon, left behind at the churchyard when the Powder Creek men came looking for trouble, had been brought to the McQuillans' gate, where it waited, stately as a glass carriage come to fetch a princess back to her castle.

Tristan helped his bride up into the seat and then climbed up beside her. He released the brake with one foot and whistled to the team, and they were on their way home.

Twilight was falling when they arrived. Emily got down without waiting for help and hurried toward the house, while Tristan took care of the team and wagon. In a backward glance, Emily saw to her consternation that he was smiling to himself.

Mr. Polymarr and Fletcher were present at the evening meal, as usual, the man oblivious to the charge in the air, the boy awkwardly aware. Tristan ate slowly, moderately, without saying much, as he would have on any other night, but his eyes followed Emily while she pushed her food around on her plate with the back of a fork. And when she got up, in desperation, to begin a clamorous round of clearing and cleaning.

"Come on, old man," Fletcher said, when Polymarr would have settled back to light a pipe. "Let's go out and make sure them Injuns is mindin' the sheep the way they should."

Mildly befuddled, Mr. Polymarr rose, thanked Emily for a fine supper, and trundled outside. Fletcher lingered a moment, his color high, glancing from Emily to Tristan and back again.

"Good night," Tristan said, and while there was a point to his words, he did not speak unkindly. Emily thought he looked like some sort of pagan priest in the flickering light of the kerosene lantern behind him, in command of a rustic magic all his own.

Fletcher nodded once and fled, and for a moment Emily's heart followed him, sore with sympathy. He was so young, and could not know that the hurt he felt would soon melt away, like a mist at sunrise.

She took up the rest of the plates and utensils.

"Sit down, Emily," Tristan said quietly. "I don't expect you to wait on me like a servant."

She had already put dishwater on the stove to heat—the reservoir was nearly empty— and now she added soap and swirled it around once before adding dirty plates. Aware of Tristan in every part of her body and spirit, she turned to him at last, using the apron around her waist to dry her hands.

He patted the bench beside him. "Come here," he said.

Over by the fire, Spud gave an expansive, contented sigh. He was old, had spent his days working hard, and he deserved the easy life of a pet.

Emily patted her hair, as though it were elaborately coiffed instead of wound into a simple plait, then forced herself across the room. Now it would begin, the wooing, the seduction he had promised to accomplish. She sat on the very edge of the bench and held her breath, like someone about to be branded with a hot iron.

Tristan traced the outlines of her cheeks with the backs of his fingers. "Did he hurt you?" he asked.

She was taken aback by the question and for the briefest of moments she had no idea what he meant. Then it came to her that he was talking about Cyrus, about her previous marriage. She shook her head. "No," she whispered.

"Then why are you so scared?"

She let out a shaky breath. His caress, innocent though it was, ignited fires in the farthest reaches of her being, and echoes of heat boomeranged to consume her at the core.

"Lots of reasons," she said. A sweet tremor went through her as he ran the pad of his thumb lightly across her lower lip, as though preparing the way for a kiss.

A smile flirted with his mouth, flew upward into his knowing eyes. "Such as?" he prompted.

She wanted to look away, but found she couldn't. She was under his spell, as surely as a mongoose facing a cobra. Her voice came out scratchy. "You might— I've never done this before—"

He leaned toward her. "I might—what?" A whisper, nothing more.

She felt the blood rush to her face and pound there like thunder beating hard against the sky. "Be disappointed," she blurted miserably.

He chuckled. "That's not likely," he said, and kissed her lightly, teasingly, on the mouth. He stood, and what was a relief to Emily was also a tearing-away. "I've got a few things to do outside, then I'm going down to the spring to wash up." He glanced at the clock ticking loudly on the mantelpiece. "I'll be about an hour, I reckon."

Emily knotted her hands together in her lap and nodded. Tristan wouldn't be sleeping in the barn that night, or in the spare room, and he was reminding her of their agreement. They would share a marriage bed, and she was free to spurn his affections—if she could.

And now she wasn't even certain that she wanted to. What sort of woman was she? She had not known Tristan Saint-Laurent a full week, and husband or no, he was a virtual stranger.

She sat at the table for a long while, torn between running away and offering herself to Tristan like a wanton. In the end, she compromised and took the middle ground. She cleaned up the kitchen, went upstairs to the master bedroom and lighted the lamp on the bedside table. She wondered, as she stripped off her clothes in a corner of the room, whether or not Tristan could see the window, glowing with welcome, from wherever he was.

After a careful washing, she donned a prim nightgown, one of the garments Aislinn had given her, and carefully hung her bright yellow wedding dress from a peg on the wall. She had brushed her teeth and was lying in bed, waiting and reflecting on the events of the day, when the door opened and Tristan came in.

She drew the covers up under her nose and peered at him over the edge.

He grinned, kicking off one boot, then the other. His hair was damp and freshly brushed and even in the dim light, his eyes sparkled with mischief and amusement. Behind the sparkle, however, blue embers smoldered, just waiting to burst into a conflagration. "Tired?" he asked, as companionably as if they were an old couple who'd shared the same bed every night for years.

"Yes," she said, her voice muffled by the covers. Her gaze tracked Tristan as he unbuckled the gunbelt and crossed the room to set it on the bedside table beside the lamp, the .45 protruding ominously from the holster. Then he pushed down his suspenders, very methodically, and she noticed that his shirt was moist in front, where he'd splashed his bare chest with water and put the garment back on without using a towel. She did not dare to look at his trousers.

"Hmmm," he said, and pulled the shirt off over his head. After tossing that away, he reached for the buckle of his belt.

Emily commanded herself to avert her eyes, and found she could not. His chest and shoulders were overwhelming enough; she did not need to see the rest of him to know that he was as magnificent, as inherently masculine, as any stallion, wild or otherwise.

He stepped back from the side of the bed to push his trousers down over his hips, and Emily caught her breath. He was erect, and his size was intimidating; far out of proportion, she was certain, to its natural counterpart, her own feminine passage. Her eyes skittered to his face and she saw that he was utterly without self-consciousness; his expression was confident, but not arrogant, and amusement touched one corner of his mouth. He was, to Emily's consternation, glorious.

He turned the lamp down until the flame was almost out, and the room held more shadow than light. There was still enough illumination to see by, however.

"My turn," he said, and tossed back the covers to reveal Emily's nightgowned figure.

He made a tsk-tsk sound with his tongue. "Unfair. Here I stand, wearing what God gave me and nothing else, while you're swathed to the throat in flannel."

Emily waxed defensive. "You didn't say I had to be—to be *naked*. You said we were going to lie down together, that's all."

"Take off the nightgown, Emily," he said patiently. "Let me look at you."

She squeezed her eyes shut and tugged at the nightgown, baring her ankles, then her knees, then her thighs...

Tristan stretched out beside her, and her knuckles went white, her fingers full of bunched flannel. "You're headed in the right direction," he prompted mischievously. "Keep going."

She could have refused him at any time, she knew that. But there was another part of her, hungry and eager, that would not countenance retreat. She pulled and, in one long, bumbling stroke, the nightgown was off, over her head. Away.

Tristan let out a low whistle, his gaze moving over her at a leisurely pace before returning to her face. "I knew you were beautiful, Mrs. Saint-Laurent," he said gruffly, "but it turns out that you're more than that. You're perfect."

Emily's throat was tight, and tears burned along her lower lashes. She had never heard such words before, from anyone, and they were an elixir, mending tiny, forgotten fractures within, though there was something else she wanted him to say. "This seduction," she said. "Does it involve touching?"

Tristan's grin flashed. "Oh, yes. Considerable touching," he assured her. Then, as gently as he might take up an injured bird, he cupped her left breast in the palm of his hand. "Like this, for instance."

Emily let out a soft moan as he teased the nipple into a hard point with his thumb. Feverishly, she reached up to put her arms around his neck and draw him down to her mouth for the first of a series of ever-deepening kisses. All the while, he continued to fondle and caress her breast, rousing a new and piercing desire that was as elemental as lightning.

When he lowered his golden head and took her nipple full into his mouth, she cried out in a sort of exultant protest, plunging splayed fingers into his hair, pressing him closer. He nibbled, then tongued, then suckled her, and when she flung both hands back onto the pillow in surrender, he caught them together at the wrists and held them gently above her head. He made free with both her breasts then, until she was tossing on the mattress, needing more, and still more—without quite knowing what it was that she needed.

He lowered a hand to the nest of moist curls at the apex of her thighs, parted her, and began a light, swirling motion with his fingers. Fire shot through Emily; she might have come back from the frantic stupor he'd induced by enjoying her breasts so thoroughly, but she was utterly lost in that moment.

He buried his face in her hair, his lips close

to her ear. "This," he said hoarsely, "is why it's worth a little pain the first time. Remember this when I take you, darlin'. Remember how it feels, and how it will be again."

With that, he kissed his way down her breastbone, pausing briefly at her belly, then proceeded to the place he had awakened to aching alertness. When he took her into his mouth, she was so stunned by the swift, searing pleasure, by the unexpectedness of the gesture itself, that she made a sound as wild and fierce as the cry of a she-wolf, half defiance, half submission.

He worked her until she begged, until she hurled her hips upward off the bed to meet him, until her entire body was slick with perspiration and her hair clung in tendrils to her cheeks, her forehead, her neck. Then, with a few teasing flicks of his tongue, he sent her reeling, tumbling, end over end, into an inferno bright enough to blind her, hot enough to brand her forever, as his and his alone.

For a time, she was one with her own heartbeat, then there came a cataclysmic explosion, following which she was borne skyward upon a pillar of fire, only to descend slowly, slowly, in scattered, burning fragments. During the long fall, Tristan comforted her, held her, whispered sweet, senseless words against her damp temple. Transported, she was at the same time excruciatingly aware of the weight, heat and substance of his body, pressed against hers. Promising other, greater odysseys, deeper mysteries, still more breathless heights to be scaled.

She clung to him and wept, for she had never suspected that such pleasure, such abandon, was possible. He soothed her, stroking her gently along the curving length of her side, murmuring, occasionally kissing her eyelids, the hollow of her throat, her forehead and temples.

After a very long time, she settled back inside her own skin, and Tristan's shadowed face came into craggy focus. The flame in the lamp on the bedside table was struggling, about to gutter out.

He kissed her mouth lightly, briefly, but in a way that reawakened the needs he had so thoroughly assuaged before. "Well," he said, in a husky voice, "did it work?"

Emily knew what he meant—he wanted to know if his attempt to seduce her had succeeded. She stretched and crooned, rested, ready for another breathless climb. "Oh, yes," she said, and wriggled against him, reveling in what she had wrought. He was not the only one who could cause physical havoc, after all; the proof of his desire pulsed between them.

"You understand what I'm asking you, Emily?" he pressed, and she loved him all the more—yes, loved him—for his concern, for his restraint, which she knew was hardwon. "I want to take you, right now, and it's probably going to hurt some. There's no way around that."

"It can't hurt more than needing you does," she reasoned, drawing his head down for a hungry kiss.

He positioned himself, paused briefly to give her a chance to change her mind, then delved into her with a long, deep stroke. And there was some pain, though short-lived and, as the friction built, so did Emily's responses, and soon she had given herself up, once again, to the primitive forces that made her entirely female. Tristan, too, was lost, and as their bodies interlocked in ferocious pleasure, their spirits took wing, like magnificent birds, soaring into the star-speckled sky.

EPILOGUE

ONE YEAR LATER...

THE BIG HOUSE WAS FILLED with light and music, and while the band—three fiddlers, a piano player and a washboard man—held forth, couples from farms and ranches for miles around danced round and round the big parlor. The furniture that usually graced that room had been carried out into the front yard, under a clear, starry sky, where children of varying dispositions and ages played house, musical chairs and tag.

Folks were still getting used to calling the ranch the Double Crescent, rather than Powder Creek, but all agreed that the place had benefited by changing hands. Tristan Saint-Laurent was making it pay, and to virtually everybody's relief, the missus had gotten shut of those sheep of hers, in midsummer, selling some, shearing some, and giving the rest to Black Eagle in trade for elk meat, herbal medicines and the odd bit of beadwork. Not that the sheep had really been so bad, for they hadn't eaten so much as a blade of range grass.

Now that Mrs. Saint-Laurent, she was a pure fascination, just like the marshal's wife, Mrs.

McQuillan. Both of them in the family way and neither one making the slightest effort to retire from public view until their confinement was over. The two women were the closest of friends, but they were also part of the community, speaking up at town meetings and clamoring for the vote.

As for the brothers, Tristan and Shay, well, they were so alike that it was nigh unto impossible to tell them apart. Once in a while, Tristan would put on Shay's badge and serve a whole week as marshal, with nobody the wiser until they chose to let the word get out. The women, Emily and Aislinn that is, could always recognize their own husbands, and claimed they were as different as any other pair of brothers. Just about anybody else in Prominence, Miss Dorrie McQuillan included, would have disagreed.

There were lots of rumors about Tristan, for by virtue of his growing up away, he was a stranger. Some said he'd been a bounty hunter once, some said a Texas Ranger, and some even maintained that he was one of the worst outlaws ever to strap on a gunbelt. The speculations had spiced up more than one conversation, and made for a favorite topic at the feed-and-grain and around the potbellied stove in the general store. Some of the old-timers said there'd be gunslingers along to challenge him, but so far none had appeared. Most people figured it would take a pure fool to mess with him or Shay, given their obvious prowess with those .45s they always wore. Funny thing, that—the way they'd grown up apart and still turned out pretty much the same.

Now, on the night of the party, the parlor crowd cleared, and Tristan Saint-Laurent and his beautiful Emily took the floor for a waltz, soon to be joined by Shay McQuillan and the lovely Aislinn. They seemed to glow, the four of them, each couple gazing into one another's eyes, as if oblivious to the rest of the world.

It was enough to make a person believe in fairy tales.